A BOHEMIAN YOUTH

Writings from an Unbound Europe

JOSEF HIRŠAL

A BOHEMIAN YOUTH

Translated by Michael Henry Heim

NORTHWESTERN UNIVERSITY PRESS

EVANSTON, ILLINOIS

Northwestern University Press
Evanston, Illinois 60208-4210

Originally published in Czech under the title *Píseň mládí*.
Copyright © 1991 by Josef Hiršal. English translation copyright © 1997 by
Michael Henry Heim. Published 1997. All rights reserved.

Printed in the United States of America

ISBN 0-8101-1223-X (cloth)
ISBN 0-8101-1592-1 (paper)

Library of Congress Cataloging-in-Publication Data

Hiršal, Josef, 1920–
   [Píseň mládí. English]
   A Bohemian youth / Josef Hiršal ; translated by Michael Henry Heim.
      p.   cm. — (Writings from an unbound Europe)
   ISBN 0-8101-1223-X (cloth : alk. paper).—ISBN 0-8101-1592-1 (pbk. : alk. paper)
   I. Heim, Michael Henry. II. Title. III. Series.
PG5038.H525P5713   1997
891.8′6354—dc21   97-40411
                                                             CIP

A WORD TO THE WISE

BE NOT DISMAYED, GENTLE READER, AT THE UNCOMMON FORM of this simple burlesque, which may put your patience to the test. Should you rise to the occasion, you are the ideal reader, the answer to a writer's prayer. Should you, however, experience difficulties following the brief basic text together with the notes, and the notes together with the notes to the notes, you are a Sunday reader and risk deriving as little from the opusculum, eager though it be to offer up its meaning, as from a timetable.

In the hope of setting out evanescent events and reminiscences and age-old tales exactly as they have surfaced in my, alas, ever more failing memory, I have perhaps erred excessively in favor of an approach I feel best suits my intention and talents.

These remarks are by no means meant as an excuse; they are more a tribute to the first type of reader and a possible guide to the second:

Begin by reading the text all the way through, and should any of the episodes catch your fancy or should you feel the need to verify one or another of the particulars, you may establish what binds them *ex post,* that is, after perusing them in their entirety. You will thus pass from the lyrico-grotesque whole, which was and remains the expression of the author's intention, to individual epic or factographical details, which I trust will not be devoid of a certain charm even on their own.

Wishing you a pleasant read, I remain,

Your Grateful Author

Wrapped in a mesh of maxims and beliefs and all that comes with them. Dragging all that comes with them behind me. The moment I move everything moves, whole you might say districts of what I drag behind me start moving. Whole districts of what I drag start speaking you might say more and more districts start moving more and more districts start speaking. Enfolding me. Tangling up. Stretching tight. Pulling, snapping, dragging, hanging. I stop short and it all moves through me. I lie down and it all moves over me. Do I play any part whatsoever? Groping my way I signal my presence by what I drag behind me. I continue to signal my presence.

A Novel

I

I am a story.

II

I am somebody's story.

III

Somebody whose story I am is the story I am.
I am somebody who is a story.

IV

I do not tell stories. I am told.
And as I am told what there is to be told is told.

Helmut Heissenbüttel
Textbuch 2 (1955–60)

■ □ ■ □ ■

MY PARENTS WERE MARRIED IN FEBRUARY 1919, as soon as Father was demobilized.[1] The wedding was reputed to have featured much food[2] and many guests, including the bandmaster[3] under whom Father had served throughout the war and who had kept him out of action, thereby assuring him a relatively easy stint.[4] The marriage greetings are still somewhere back in Chomutice in one of those little chests painted in the Moravian-Slovak folk style,[5] and as a child I would enjoy going through them. The one I liked best was the one sent by a merchant named Jelínek, who later, when I was an adolescent, was called before the Jičín court for pederasty[6] and who did in fact solicit prepubescent boys for the purpose of mutual masturbation.[7] The greeting read as follows: "May blossoms of bliss and stars of peace accompany you on the true path. Antonín Jelínek and family." Then there was a greeting inscribed on parchment in supposedly old-fashioned script and decorated with a large seal.[8] It was humorous in a gossipy kind of way[9] and was composed by Kozel,[10] the baker, though officially it came from the Sokol Gymnastic Society,[11] to which both my parents belonged.[12] Later, during the war, the same Kozel appears to have written a letter to the district authorities denouncing Father for slaughtering a pig on the sly.[13] The less than conclusive evidence was the handwriting in the denunciation letter,[14] which was shown to Father by a decent fellow, a Czech, whose job it was to look into the affair and who swept it under the carpet.[15] I was less taken with the rest of the greetings. Josef, the groom, was twenty-six at the time, Anežka, his bride, née Vydrová, twenty-two.[16] Father was still living with his mother, whom the newlyweds both called Mother,[17] in a small house in Chomutičky.[18] Uncle Václav, Father's elder stepbrother,[19] a member of the Czech Legionnaires,[20] was still somewhere in Siberia,[21] but when my mother moved into her mother-in-law's house she found another tenant there, an odd young girl my grandmother had taken in during the war to allay her fear of sleeping alone and to keep her spirits up. The girl's name was Fanda Vávrová.[22] She showed no sign of moving out after the wedding and had to be asked point-blank to leave,[23] after which the three were left on their own with two cows, a pig, a goat, several chickens, and three geese.[24] The house was divided into a large room—where they lived,[25] cooked, and slept—and a small room, which had nothing in it but an old piano made by J. Baumbach, Wien,[26] and bought by Father before the war from Mr. Javůrka, the organist,[27] for a hundred gulden. Where he found the money for it I cannot say.[28] It always had a flugelhorn, a trumpet, and a violin[29] lying on it. Those were the instruments Father played. The family worked in the fields.[30] We started with just under three acres and had a bit added on as a result of the postwar agricultural reform. Mother probably received a piece of land as part of her dowry as well. By the time I was a boy, it came to just over six acres plus a half-acre of meadowland.[31] On Saturdays and Sundays[32] Father played the violin and trumpet for parties, dances, pilgrimages, and church fairs. He was also a concert flugelhorn soloist or *Soloflügelhornist,* as his profession was officially called during the Monarchy.[33] The family was therefore quite well off. Besides, Father had been promised the post of organist at the Church of Saint Dionysius[34] in Chomutice by the parish priest, František Melich,[35] who eventually became a dean and a monsignor, a kind of privy councilor to the Pope. The post came with a piece of church land and a steady income from funerals and weddings. But promises are made to be broken, and because Father was active on the Sokol board[36] the priest decided against him and hired first a Mr. Veselka and then a Mr. Valtera.[37] In other words, Father had to make do without it. All that remained of his hopes was a bronze plaque with the inscription "Josef Hiršal, Choirmaster," which he had had made somewhere in Jičín or Hořice with uncharacteristic pride. I was an adolescent when I discovered it in the drawer of the bedside table in the big room.[38] The wedding took place on the 19th of February in the parish church at Chomutice with Father Melich officiating and the above-mentioned Veselka playing the organ. Father Melich ordered Veselka to play free of charge because Father had done so much for the church.[39] I was born in July 1920, that is to say, seventeen months later. I had a Catholic baptism, my godfathers being Mother's brother Pepík[40] and Father's stepbrother Václav,[41] both of whom had served in the Legion and had recently returned from Siberia. Everyone said it was a gala affair, though for years afterward people talked about how my uncle and god-father Pepík passed up the delicacies for soft cheese sandwiches.[42] Still, the baptism was nothing compared with the birth. I wanted to come out feet first! Emilie Vávrová[43] the mid-wife—no relation to the above-mentioned Fanda—couldn't cope and had to send to Obora for Dr. Dostál,[44] a well-known alco-holic.[45] He got me out, but I refused to breathe. For two hours he tossed me up to the ceiling, but I failed to respond. He was about to give up on me when I caught my breath and let out a cry.[46] I was named Josef Václav after both my godfathers. They are the names of my father and grandfather as well. The number twenty-four played an unusual part in all this. I was born on the twenty-fourth in a house with the number twenty-four. One of my godfathers lived in house number twenty-four at Chomutice, the other in house number twenty-four at Chomutičky. Both Mother and Father were born in houses with the number twenty-four, and there were supposedly twenty-four guests at the baptism. It was predicted that the number twenty-four would have fateful consequences for me. It did not. What did were years ending in eight: 28, 38, 48, 58, 68, 78.[47] I remember nothing of the time immediately following my birth. My first memory, which is actually the memory of a memory, dates from when I was two. I was standing on a little green stool in one of my dresses[48] when there was a knock at the door. Mother and I were at home alone. Mother called out, "Come in!" and in came the maid of the Kazda family[49] from Chomutice and said, "My mistress the schoolteacher's wife she asked me to give you this honey here for the little boy." Whereupon she handed Mother a small jar. Not knowing which little boy she had in mind, I was terribly jealous until Mother spooned out a dollop of honey for me.[50] She then put it away in the cupboard. Another memory of a memory dates from when I was about three. I woke up terrified one morning and cried out, "Look,

Mama! What's wrong with me!" It was an in-fantile erection—my first.[51] Mother took one look at my cockadoo, as we called it then, and said, "Oh, it's nothing." And in fact before long my tiny member had returned to its—alas—normal state. The third event lodged in my memory took place at about the same time, the spring of 1923. My parents were either plowing or sowing the Hill Field,[52] and I was lying in the grass on the border of our land next to Anda Jiranová, a girl from a poor family and my elder by two years.[53] I must have been playing with my cockadoo because I asked to see hers. "Girls haven't got cockadoos," she said. "Girls have cunts.[54] Go and tell your mama." And off she ran. So instead of seeing what I had so hoped to see,[55] I toddled up through the clumps of soft dirt to relay the message to Mama. Father stopped the cows[56] when he saw me coming, and when I told him what I had to say he brandished his whip in Anda's direction. I had a strict upbringing.[57]

■ □ ■ □ ■

NOTES

1. Father reported for duty with the Eleventh Regiment at Jičín in the spring of 1915 and was soon sent to Sopron for basic training.[1] Even before it was over, however, the bandmaster had him assigned to the military band.[2] During the war he followed his regiment to the Russo-Polish province of Galicia and—as he put it—"to Italy in the Tyrol."[3] He returned on *Urlaub*[4] in August 1918 and was due to return to his regiment in the field six weeks before the war came to an end. Instead, he waited it out in Chomutičky, not reporting back to Jičín until after the Monarchy had fallen. His regiment was then transferred to Dolní Kubín in Slovakia, but he was demobilized early, in January 1919, when he was discovered to have a tubercular lung cavity.[5]

2. Even though basic foodstuffs were still in short supply, we had all kinds of delicacies: Grandmother—Father's mother—had a pig slaughtered,[1] and Mother's parents in Chomutice killed a calf. And because Grandmother and Grandfather Vydra were butter and egg merchants, traveling from village to village[2] and selling what they bought in the Old Town market in Prague,[3] we always had the makings for cakes.

3. The bandmaster, whose name was Karel Kastner,

came from Jičín.[1] During the war Grandmother supplied his family—his wife and son—with variously acquired comestibles so that he would pull strings for Father. He got into the band because Bandmaster Kastner had heard him playing bugle calls and invited him to audition.[2] Father was a fine musician. Music ran in the family on his father's side: his father, who died in 1905, was a stonecutter and bandmaster. My father had studied trumpet, flugelhorn, and violin from childhood and passed the audition with flying colors, but his captain refused to put through the transfer and the bandmaster had to appeal to the colonel, who finally gave permission.[3] Though not particularly robust, Father was generally considered a good soldier, but the captain had another reason for opposing the transfer: Father's knowledge of German made him constantly useful.[4] While in the band, he made friends with Václav Soukup from Běchary,[5] who also played the flugelhorn, and a violinist whose name I do not know but who was a German and concertmaster for the Prussian crown prince[6] and spent his evenings practicing scales with Father.

4. Band members were exempt from all military obligations but setting up roadblocks.[1] Father often told the story of how one day he was in a ditch ramming some dirt when there was a burst of machine-gun fire and an alert. A friend, who had been setting up a camouflage net on the road, tumbled into the ditch for cover. After the alert Father realized his friend had been hit between the eyes. He was dead.[2] Otherwise Father had a grand old time in the army. He was the bandmaster's pet. Even when under excep-

tional circumstances other band members had to go on guard, he would peacefully copy out music or transcribe parts for various instruments.[3]

5. The chest had a black lacquer finish with white-red-yellow-blue apples, roses, and other designs painted on it. Uncle Pepík had brought it back from Moravian Slovakia before the war.[1] Besides marriage greetings it housed the family jewels: a pair of large wedding rings with the newlyweds' initials and the date 19 February 1919 engraved on them, plus two other rings with white and red stones. While a student, I expropriated first one then the other, selling them to Moravec, the Jičín goldsmith.[2] I spent part of the money on various dainties and lost the other part in card games like *capári* and *ferbl.*[3]

6. Antonín Jelínek, who had a grain and grocery business but also served beer on tap, was denounced by a local schoolmaster, Jaroslav Koťátko,[1] who supplied him with a fourteen-year-old gardener's apprentice named Gabriel as bait. Koťátko was motivated by their mutual antipathy and perhaps by obscure machinations, Jelínek being both chairman of the local school board[2] and head alderman and Koťátko a highly ambitious teacher bent on a career in local government. Be that as it may, there was no boy in the village who, upon reaching the age of fourteen, had not been subject to Jelínek's attentions. Some he would tempt with chocolates or fruit drops, others with driving lessons—he was one of the few people we knew who owned a car, a Zet.[3] Everyone called him Pansy, while his farmer brother Josef—the two were not on

speaking terms[4]—was known as Josef the Humper because of an affair he was carrying on in his hayloft.[5]

7. Jelínek was a skilled psychologist and used different techniques on each boy. I, for example, was promised typing lessons in his office;[1] Pepík Stich[2] was taken to the steam baths in Hradec Králové; Vaněk Fišera,[3] known for his sweet tooth, got a fifty-heller coin and a chocolate bar; Franta Tázler[4] was given a personal demonstration of the Zet motor; and Herbert Špigl[5] went on a two-day trip with him to Prague, during which Jelínek let him take over the wheel, pulled down his trousers—Herbert said his underpants went all the way to his knees—and tossed himself off, thereby risking an accident and a nasty court case. When he was in fact called before the court, the responses were varied. "I mean, how low can you stoop!" said old man Okrouhlický,[6] while Mr. Rubín[7] the postman cried out indignantly, "So that's what you get for years of public service!" As for Father, he gave his black mustache[8] a twirl, shook his head wisely, and said, "Call it an illness if you like. Still, he shouldn't have done it."

8. It was written in bright blue pseudo-Gothic characters on translucent paper. Not real parchment, no; the kind of paper my grandfather used for wrapping butter (the kind you dipped into water before using) and we called "butter paper."[1] The seal was round and red with the Sokol Gymnastic Society logo on it.

9. Unfortunately the text itself is not available. The content was more or less as follows: two old women were observed under the chestnut tree near the church

whispering about how Sokol Brother Josef and Sokol Sister Anežka were about to tie the knot, and soon a flock of little Sokols would emerge from the nest and join the ranks of the Society,[1] etc.

10. Kozel the baker moved to Chomutice from the village of Lány, near Bělohrad, before the war. He had a big belly and three children. His son Eda got a girl from Ohnišťany pregnant and was forced to marry at the age of sixteen.[1] His daughter Jiřina, who was considered a beauty, sang at the feasts of Saint Nicholas and Saint Sylvester and played romantic leads in operettas.[2] Then there was Ruda, the second son, who was a bit of a simpleton.[3] Kozel later became mayor,[4] but was removed from office for dipping into the town's electricity budget. Every morning he donned a clean white apron with JK embroidered in red on it and made the rounds of the drinking establishments,[5] taking a snort of beer or the hard stuff at each. He was eventually discovered to have paid for the drinks out of public funds.[6] Otherwise he was much loved and always good for a laugh. While he was out and around, the bakery was manned by his apprentice Franta Tonar, a feebleminded lad who made it through only three years of school and died young of softening of the brain.[7]

11. The local branch of the Sokol Gymnastic Society was founded in 1906.[1] Its first event was neither gymnastic nor patriotic but rather a New Year's Eve celebration with printed invitations and all kinds of festivities. I found the invitation among Father's papers. It read: "Gala New Year's Party Italiano! Vino! Beero! All You Can Eato!"[2]

12. Mother and Father joined the Sokol Society a few years after the Chomutice branch was founded. Mother took part in several of the local and national gymnastic events;[1] Father served primarily in an administrative capacity, though he also contributed his skills as a musician, rehearsing songs with rank amateurs for talent shows, accompanying rhythmic exercises on the violin and piano, and conducting the orchestra for various cultural events. Fučík's "Marinarella"[2] almost invariably figured on the program.

13. Slaughtering pigs on the sly was common practice during World War II. This is how it was done: The breeder would buy a piglet[1] and slaughter a full-grown hog. When the inspector came, he would say he had a runt in the stall, a freak of nature.[2] Some of the more dramatically inclined breeders would put on a show, driving the piglet out into the courtyard, bemoaning their lot, offering the puny specimen to the inspector free of charge, cursing the sow that gave birth to it, and so on. They usually got away with it too, though a village might have as many as twenty runts at a time. All it took were a few sausages and a slice of ham for the inspector.[3]

14. Father never actually claimed that Kozel had written the letter. The z was suspicious, however, the baker's cursive version of the letter being quite distinctive.[1] Since he had no reason to believe the man his enemy, the act could have been motivated only by a temporary mental imbalance.[2] And in fact, it occurred just after he had been dismissed as mayor. Yet Father had no hand whatever in the affair.

15. By and large Czech civil servants and police officials behaved patriotically, and when it came to investigating economic crimes their patriotism paid off. They would first report to the local authorities and have the mayor send his constable or even his child to notify the suspect. Šimák the shoemaker, who was mayor at the time and on none too good terms with Father,[1] sent his apprentice. Father immediately moved the vat he used for curing the meat from the storage room to the attic and hid it under some straw. There was no search, however. The inspector showed Father the anonymous letter and asked him whether he recognized the handwriting; they wanted to "make it hard on the guy who did it for trying to put one over on them."[2] Father claimed not to recognize it, though he told Mother later "it looked like Kozel's."

16. My parents had known each other for a long time—almost ten years—before they married. Mother, aged thirteen, was on her way home with a new scrubbing brush. It was summer. She was barefoot. Father, a seventeen-year-old shoemaker's apprentice,[1] went up to her, grabbed the brush out of her hand, and scraped her bare calves with it. Mother ran home in tears. Thus began a friendship that turned into profound love. Their shared affection grew even more intense during the war. Father reported for duty in 1915 and wrote to Mother—his dear Agička—three times a week; she answered him once or twice a week.[2] Before the war Mother's parents, who were not particularly happy with the friendship, had sent her to Prague to take service with a teacher's family in the Nusle district.[3] The teacher's name was Šedivý. She did not

last long there. To the Šedivýs' disappointment—they liked her very much—she begged her mother to take her home: she missed her chickens and geese.

17. Grandmother was widowed in 1905. Grandfather, a stonecutter and bandmaster, was said to have died of tuberculosis, though it was more likely silicosis.[1] He married Grandmother in 1892, having lost his first wife, with whom he had a son, my Uncle Václav, to consumption two years earlier. Grandmother was born out of wedlock.[2] Her mother came from a family of Třtěnice landowners who sent her packing when she told them she was pregnant. She hired herself out as a maid to peasants, then worked for a time on a stud farm, and for the rest of her life she used the German word for stallion, *Hengst*.[3] She took little Aninka everywhere she went and never married. Grandmother attended school in Třtěnice.[4] Then she, too, worked as a maid. Her life was not particularly hard. She was employed by the Khans, a family of Jewish grocers in Chomutice.[5] One day, as she tells it, they heard the funeral bell toll and Mrs. Khan said, "Have you heard who died? Hiršal's young wife.[6] You know, Hiršal would make you a good husband." Which he did.

18. Grandmother moved to Chomutičky after her marriage.[1] Having amassed a small nest egg, she was able to contribute a cow to Grandfather's chattels. On Thursdays and Fridays Grandfather hewed tombstones[2]—on Thursdays and Fridays because on Saturdays he went off to perform with his band and was likely to tarry.[3] The boys he gave music lessons to would go from village to village and pub to pub looking for him.[4] Apparently he had never touched a drop

of alcohol before his second marriage.[5] If he did not return by Wednesday, Grandmother would go from pub to pub herself and drag him home.[6] She had to cut through fields and meadows because the moment Grandfather sensed a tap in the vicinity he wanted to stop. Grandmother would let him have one drink, and when they got home he was ready to fall into bed. By Thursday morning he was back to normal and stonecutting.[7] Childhood experiences such as these made his son—my father—a teetotaler for life.

19. Uncle Václav was never the apple of Grandmother's eye.[1] Grandfather wanted him to be a stonecutter and Father to study sculpture at Hořice. Nothing came of either plan. Uncle Václav never took to stonecutting;[2] he became a mason instead.[3] He left home before completing his apprenticeship and moved in with a family by the name of Sobotka. He was quite a drinker, and when Grandfather died, the owner of a local pub, a man by the name of Antoš,[4] showed up with a Jičín lawyer and carried off his part of the inheritance.[5]

20. Uncle Václav entered the army before Father and was taken prisoner at the Russian front in 1917. He did not join the Legion until the autumn of 1918, however, working in a Russian factory in the interim.[1] He feared reprisals by the Austrians in the highly unlikely case the Central Powers should win the war.[2]

21. Uncle Václav came home from his "anabasis" with the Legionnaires via Vladivostok in the spring of 1920. He brought back his uniform, a gun (which we kept at home[1] until the German Occupation, when

Father buried it in the garden), and a green silk handkerchief with the Czechoslovak insignia and "Souvenir of the Czechoslovak Legion in Russia" printed on it. Soon after his return Father taught him to play the double bass and the helicon, thus enabling him to supplement his earnings as a mason. A year later he married Mother's sister Marie, whose other serious suitor, Petřivý the postman, had shot himself upon learning he was mortally ill (the apices of his lungs had been tainted with consumption). After marrying, Uncle Václav moved to Chomutice and the house Mother had been born in. Apparently his interest in Marie antedated the war, but Grandfather had refused him her hand because of his drinking and card playing. He was naturally thrilled to give her hand to a Legionnaire.[2]

22. Fanda Vávrová was an orphan. She had never actually moved in, nor did she help in the fields. For plowing, harrowing, sowing, and harvesting Grandmother was given two soldiers. One was a prisoner of war, a Bosnian by the name of Periša, the other an invalid, an outpatient from the military hospital at Chomutice, a Hungarian whose surname I do not know. He left behind a white handkerchief, which I discovered in Grandmother's chest as a boy. It had three stars and the name Lajos embroidered on it.[1]

23. Mother, though usually quite timid, asked her to leave. She then slept at her godmother's, an old woman by the name of Laloušková.[1] Though unwed for years, she eventually married Splítek the blacksmith.[2]

24. The second cow came with Mother's dowry. We thus had an offside cow and a nearside cow. When we

rode out into the fields, Father would spur them on with a "Gee, Off!" I never heard him say, "Gee, Near!" The house was made of wood, and the gable had a cross with a figure of Christ on it.[1]

25. The big room had two beds in it. I slept in one, Grandmother in the other.[1] It also had a bench, a table, four chairs, a buffet, and a large tile stove. The tiles were a grayish blue, and the ones nearest the fire had an unearthly glow to them. The stove was built just after Grandmother's wedding by a stove-maker from Nevrátice by the name of Maximilián.[2] It replaced a modest potbellied stove of cast iron. For buns and cakes, and perhaps meat and poultry as well, she used the ovens belonging to our neighbors the Dobešes, Vodičkas, or Splíteks.

26. The piano was built in about 1870.[1] It was tuned quite low, the A being nearly a G-sharp. Father played it all the time. He especially enjoyed accompanying singers practicing for performances at musicals, Sokol events, Christmas parties, and the firemen's New Year's balls.[2] I could pick out a few tunes but nothing serious. Father's attempts to give me lessons failed miserably. Classical music was beyond me. The music on the piano tended to be pieces like Rudolf Friml's early "Vagabond Songs" or routines from the Seven of Hearts cabaret in Prague.[3]

27. Father owed a great deal to Javůrek, a man approximately ten years his senior. Javůrek not only taught him to play the organ but also initiated him into the mysteries of harmony and theory, which meant that when he became a bandmaster he was able to arrange pieces on the basis of their melody alone.[1]

Father even tried his hand at composition, setting a decadent poem by the name of "Morbid Wasteland Blossoms" to music.[2] Just before the First World War Javůrek moved to Třebechovice near Mount Oreb, his wife's hometown. Their first child, a boy, died young and is buried in the Chomutice cemetery.[3] Their second boy entered the Church and apparently ended up a bishop.

28. Grandmother had some savings and Father earned a bit on the side giving concerts and playing at pubs. They may also have taken out a long-term loan, though it is more probable that they bought it from Javůrek on time.

29. Father bought the flugelhorn, trumpet, and violin as soon as he finished his apprenticeship,[1] but Bílek, the bandmaster who took Grandfather's place, did not want to give him lessons. Not that he refused him outright, but whenever Father came with one of the instruments he would be told that Bílek was not at home. He was afraid that Father would eventually take over the band from him as crown prince. His fears were as unfounded as his attempts to sabotage Father's talent were unsuccessful:[2] Father simply went all the way to Stará Páka for trumpet and flugelhorn lessons. He later took organ lessons from the above-mentioned Javůrek and violin lessons from a teacher in Třtěnice, a man by the name of Haken, a future chairman of the Communist Party of Czechoslovakia.[3] Haken was fond of Father's pure tenor voice and accompanied him when he sang at various meetings.[4]

30. Even as an infant in swaddling clothes I was taken into the fields by my parents. The closest field to

our house was Hill Field,[1] which was just outside Chomutičky and was in fact on a slope overgrown with weeds. Then there was Pond Field,[2] which was on the way to Třtěnice, and Kabáty Field,[3] which was named after a hamlet belonging to the neighboring village of Vojice. The field farthest away was Woods Field,[4] which was next to a copse of oaks and beeches also known as Kabáty or, rather, Little Kabáty, Big Kabáty being a deciduous forest about half a mile down the road. The Chapel of Saint Anne, which stood halfway between them, was the site of a church feast on the third Sunday in July.[5]

31. We were given the meadow as a result of the agrarian reform promulgated by the Czechoslovak government following the First World War. It had originally been part of the Chomutičky Estate, which until the fall of the Monarchy belonged to Karl Prince Trauttmansdorff. After the war it was declared a "residual farmstead" and incorporated into the Obora Estate, which was owned first by an industrialist named Liebig from Liberec[1] and then by the Czechoslovak Sugar Society. When the Chomutičky Estate and the Obora Estate were divided again, the latter was bought by one Josef Horák, an executive at the Bank for Small Business, who embezzled the funds to purchase it, signed it over to his wife, and threw himself under the train that ran through the forest there;[2] the former was bought by a man named Rygl, the steward of an estate in Chlumec.[3] The section of it that came to us was quite small, but it had a pond and was rich in mushrooms.

32. On Sunday and Monday mornings Father "slept off" his music.[1]

33. It was a profession in which he made quite a name for himself. Bandmasters from far and wide invited him to play with them: Fišera from Nový Bydžov, Šperk from Staré Smrkovice, Ort from Starý Bydžov, Koubek from Vysoké Veselí, Rulf from Lázně Bělohrad, etc. Traveling from concert to concert, Father got to know a number of the leading figures in the world of music: the composer Karel Moor,[1] the head of the Military Conservatory Captain Mach,[2] and the composer Karel Vacek, whose father lived in Vysoké Veselí and strung Father's bows.[3] Karel Vacek himself came to see us several times and played trumpet-flugelhorn duets with Father.

34. A late Baroque church dating from the end of the eighteenth century, it was noteworthy for the curious echo beneath the chandelier and for the fresco adorning the cupola. The fresco, *A Bohemian Paradise,* is the work of the well-known painter Josef Karmoliń.[1] The figure of the devil is particularly striking: brown with sky-blue bat wings, it sits on its haunches, guilefully staring into the distance.

35. Monsignor František Melich became the parish priest at Chomutice following the First World War, his predecessor, Josef Hlavsa, having fallen in battle while serving as a chaplain at Moravská Ostrava. Hlavsa had been a fine musician and played violin duets with my Grandfather Václav in the early years of the century.[1] The Reverend Father Melich, who celebrated the fiftieth anniversary of his ordination in 1939

and remained in Chomutice after retiring from the priesthood,[2] lived to a ripe old age: he died in Jičín in the fifties. He came from the Krkonoše Mountains—from Roškopov or thereabouts—and was known for his "bitter" breakfast.[3]

36. See notes 11 and 13. Father did not have an easy time with the Sokol board what with his singing at Catholic funerals and an occasional church concert.[1] Freethinker Marie Houžvičková[2] took Sokol Brother Hiršal to task in the local weekly *Hlasy od Cidliny* (Voices from the Cidlina), accusing him of playing up to the church authorities. Her article ended: "Birds of a feather flock together. Witness the parish priest and his new organist." Father came to his own defense—and was backed by the secretary of the board, Fišera the tailor, and later perhaps by Rubín the postman as well—by pointing out that he engaged in said activities for reasons both pecuniary and musical. He also called Houžvičková a bitch, for which he got his comeuppance.[3]

37. In 1931 Valtera, the organist, opened a stationery shop in Chomutice. Besides stationery he sold newspapers, schoolbooks, and—later—toys and cigarettes. The shop occupied the ground floor of the house he had built for himself near the new school. After failing to obtain the hand of a local girl (her father, the smallholder and innkeeper Antoš, having declared he saw no reason to "put his hard-earned money into a pile of paper"), he married a rich Catholic girl from an estate in Southern Bohemia.[1] He also had a large stamp collection and was careful always to say "darn" instead of "damn."[2]

38. I had long since forgotten its existence when it surfaced after Mother's death. I used a solution of vinegar and salt to polish it.

39. See note 36. Father played the organ and the violin, and conducted the choir for midnight and high masses on Christmas and Easter, singing in Ryba's *Christmas Mass* and in the *Passion* (sometimes as the Evangelist, sometimes as Jesus). He was introduced to church music by the above-mentioned Javůrek and continued to cultivate it even when, shortly after my birth, he left the Catholic Church and—clearly under the influence of my mother and her politically progressive family—entered the newly founded Czechoslovak Church.[1] He never crossed himself or beat his chest during church services, and found sermons, litanies, and rosaries a big bore; nor did he pray at home[2] or sing religious songs in private.[3]

40. Uncle Pepík was the nicest and most generous of Mother's three brothers. He was an attorney for the Cooperative Society of the Prague Central Slaughterhouse. He always sent us a box of chocolate and fondant figurines for our Christmas tree—first with Grandmother, later with Grandfather—and when he himself came for a visit he would bring chocolate creams.[1] He married soon after his return from Siberia, having answered a classified advertisement in a Prague newspaper. Aunt Jarmila was an Academy-trained painter. The daughter of a Professor Paul, who seems to have died before the war, she came from a highly respected Prague family. Uncle Pepík's mother-in-law looked down on him and never let him forget his plebeian origins.[2] She had two daughters in addi-

tion to Aunt Jarmila—Karolinka and Tóninka—both of whom worked for a bank and never married. Besides the family house in the Vinohrady section of Prague (which Uncle Pepík did not inherit, of course, it being in the old woman's name), the family owned a piece of land in the country, in Stráňčice, and the old maids had thousands in their bank accounts.[3]

41. See notes 19, 20, and 21. I should add that Uncle Václav had three children with Aunt Mařka: Standa, Růžena, and Vláďa. The house where they lived—the house Mother was born in—was called The Verges.[1] Uncle Václav built a large barn and stable on the property. The stable housed cows, a bull, and a horse named Fuksa, which Grandfather rode through the neighboring villages when buying up eggs, butter, and poultry for the market.[2]

42. Soft cheese (also called gooey cheese, old cheese, or, in teachers' families, domestic cheese) was made by letting curds stand in a stoneware pot for a time—a week in winter, four or five days in summer—with an admixture of cumin, paprika, and salt. Spread thick on buttered bread, it is delicious.[1]

43. Emilie Vávrová, the midwife, was a local celebrity. She took a medicine bag to every delivery, and the plaque on her house read "Licensed Midwife, Assistant to Dr. Rubeška." She was talkative and good-natured and was loved by all. People called Mr. Vávra the "midhusband."

44. Dr. Jaroslav Dostál, official general practitioner for the district, lived and practiced in Obora in a building called the Old Post Office. He treated all

kinds of bumps, bruises, and maladies, looked in on difficult deliveries, and pulled teeth.[1]

45. Dr. Dostál spent all his leisure time drinking away his fees at the Jelíneks' pub. His wife was an alcoholic as well. She would have her rum brought in from the Jirans' pub, which was just across the road, sending over her daughters or son,[1] or, if they were unavailable, patients from her husband's waiting room. Dr. Dostál liked to wear white ducks, which, when drunk, he often sullied. Many a patient had helped him home in distress. Yet he was reputed an excellent doctor. He died of liver problems in 1929.

46. Dr. Dostál was a cynic, though a likable one. Family lore has it that when I came out of the womb he told my mother, "This one's a lemon. You'll need another go at it." But when I finally let out my howl, he smiled and said, "Well, well! He'll do after all."

47. In 1928 I had a B in conduct, in 1938 we had Munich, in 1948 we celebrated the Party's "Victorious February," in 1958 I lost my post as editor at the publishing house of the Union of Czechoslovak Writers and had my second kidney-stone operation, in 1968 we received our "Fraternal Aid" from the Soviet Union, and in 1978 my mother died.

48. I wore pleated woolen dresses with buttons, one of which I managed to bite off and swallow. All little boys wore dresses at the time. There was no need for nappies: you just peed. All my clothes were handed down to my younger brother Miroslav, so they are ingrained in my memory. Every time I think of them I taste honey.[1]

49. My parents were close friends with Josef Kazda (a teacher of vocational subjects who died of a brain tumor in 1933) and his wife; my brother Mirek and I were equally close to Jindra and Pepík, their children.[1] Kazda was a fine musician and often gave recitals with my father, accompanying him on the piano when he sang or played the violin.[2] He also went in for photography and bee-keeping, and did the sets and lighting for school and amateur theatricals. On holidays he was in charge of fireworks and specialized in Bengal lights. He was one of the first radio enthusiasts in the country and built his own wireless sets. He made one for us in 1925.[3] He taught penmanship, general science, physics, and chemistry at the local school, and was called Chem for short. His father was a shoemaker from Vysoké Veselí, his wife the daughter of the tax collector for the estate.[4] We loved going to their house when we were children: it was like a sorcerer's kitchen. We would take him rotten willow branches, which he used to smoke out bees.[5]

50. The taste of honey had been completely unknown to me before that. All I knew was a homemade sugarbeet treacle.[1] Later I would chew the beeswax after Mr. Kazda or our neighbor Mr. Uxa the tailor extracted as much honey as they could from the combs.[2]

51. I couldn't get over how stiff, large, and hard my member had grown. I was also surprised to see the clear outline of the glans under the foreskin. It was years before I could pull it back all the way. Although I was attentive to everything around me, I was most attentive to my own body and its responses, libidinal in particular.

---

52. See notes 30 and 30.1. The field lay close to the village and our house, and in 1924 Father toyed with the idea of putting up a barn there. He later considered building a bigger house, but decided to buy one in Chomutice instead. A good thing too,[1] even though he'd had a considerable amount of rubble stone hauled in for the foundation.

53. The Jirans were day laborers. They had two sons in addition to Anda, if I'm not mistaken, though I can't quite picture them. The family was as poor as you could be without going into the poorhouse, and therefore permanently suspect.[1]

54. That was how I first learned of the anatomical distinction between male and female and heard my first taboo word. The essentials remained veiled in secrecy until I discovered three tomes on the bookshelf. The first was *The Beauty of the Female Body,* which Father in his bachelor days had ordered directly from the publisher.[1] It featured reproductions of the naked beauties of various nations: female form against a red background, female form against a blue background, female form against a yellow, purple, green, or orange background. I later learned from an issue of *Nový lid* (The New People)[2] that the bulk of the publisher's subscribers consisted of Roman Catholic priests. The second book was *The Young Mother* and had clearly made its appearance in the family just prior to my birth. Besides the embryo in various phases and positions, it showed the female genitals. I found them strange, not to say repellent. The third was *Sexual Hygiene for Married Couples,* which my parents had acquired shortly after they were married.

It contained illustrations of both varieties of genitals.[3] Much later, in a song I heard from a drunken rookie by the name of Frantík Chmelík,[4] I learned another taboo word for the female genitalia. The song went like this: "I've got a girl in Louny; I share her with my crony. I've got a girl in Blatná; she's got a big black twat, ha!" I've never liked that word, if only for the forced rhyme.[5] I learned another word from a schoolmate named Milík Kocek,[6] who later became a police officer. It was rather odd: "piddler." I have never run across it since. And once I heard Mrs. Hejduková,[7] the wife of a schoolteacher, call out to her little daughter Libuška, who was swimming in a stream, "Cover up your quimlet, darling!"

55. When a few months later I managed to satisfy my curiosity,[1] I was rather disappointed: I didn't think she had much to show.[2]

56. Father brought the cows to a halt with a cry of "Whoa!" and a pull on the reins, shoved his hat back on his head, and gave me a dirty look.[1]

57. Sex and eroticism were taboo in our family. Both my parents kept a careful watch over my morals. Father's guidance consisted mainly of frequent threats and spankings. He also recommended corporal punishment to my teachers.[1] When he heard I'd been seen down by the pond with a certain Jarča Pluhařová—I was seventeen at the time—he declared, "If I ever catch you with her again, I'll beat the living daylights out of you. She's a dirty whore, that girl."[2]

■ □ ■ □ ■

NOTES TO THE NOTES

1.1. A town on the Hungarian side of Neusiedler Lake. It is known in Czech literature primarily for its brewery. Jaroslav Hašek mentions it in *The Good Soldier Švejk* ("The Hungarian breweries in Sopron and in Gross-Kanisza bought from my firm for their export beer, which they exported as far as Alexandria, an average of a thousand sacks of hops a year" [London: Penguin Books, 1974, p. 188]), as does Bohumil Hrabal in *Dancing Lessons for the Advanced in Age* ("so I switched from shoemaking to brewing and trained as a maltster and set off on a tour of Hungary, oh what a brewery they have in Sopron! bright red with white trimming and green windows, Tyrol style, nothing but white tile inside, and nice little ladders at every window so in case of fire the firemen can climb up and down like the monkeys in Dresden" [New York: Harcourt Brace, 1995, pp. 18–19]).

1.2. See note 3. It should be added that the name of the bandmaster's wife was Růžena and that Father's place in the bandmaster's good books was more than confirmed when on her name day he had the army chorus sing, "Sweet dreams, my Růžinka! Sweet dreams, my Růžinka! Sweet dreams, my Růžinka! Sweet dreams of me!"

1.3. Starting 14 May 1916 Father kept a war diary, recording the events, experiences, and moods of Sopron, Galicia, and the Italian Front. The following are excerpts from that diary:

1916

14 May. Sitting alone in the woods, writing to my dear Agička. Church service this morning with Hussars. No concert. Rain until one. Evening performance of operetta *All About Love*.

20 May. Morning rehearsal for concert. Afternoon rehearsal for *The Vagabond Student*. Then out with the artillery. Evening performance of the operetta *Die oder keine* after a nice time playing the piano for the men in the pub. Letter from Agička.

1 June. Church service this morning with entire regiment, then report to commander for leave. Spent the afternoon writing letters to Agička and Mama. Got food parcel. Then park concert and evening performance of the last operetta: *The Magic of the Waltz*.

19 July. Bought new flugelhorn: 90 crowns. Tested it immediately at park concert.

22 July. Played for unveiling of monument to our regiment (bust of the Emperor), then in a new villa on a hill in the woods. A good time was had by all.

1917

22 March. Fine weather riding through beautiful Hungarian countryside, Tatra foothills. Morning coffee at Új Csolna, mess at Nagy Csolna. Rested until two, wrote home. Out of sorts. Coffee at Odeberg.

10 April. Morning played for review behind lines, afternoon dug selves in. Russian aeroplane overhead; our men try and shoot it down. Letters from A. and Ruda.

15 April. Played at morning mass for First Regiment, returned for afternoon concert. Wrote letter to A. and family, a soldier on leave will deliver it. From 9:30 to 12 midnight Russian drumfire on our right flank. Terrible night, gas attack, *marschbereit*.

16 April. Sent to stand guard at 5 A.M., writing this under cover, artillery firing at us again, right flank. Back to camp at 1. Letter and card from A. dated 10 and 12 April.

———

5 June. Rude awakening 3 A.M.: shrapnel exploding at a hundred paces followed by shots flying overhead aimed at the Bavarians. Several artillerymen wounded. Our whole company and regiment officers made for the rear. Afternoon rehearsal. Letter from A. Answered immediately.

14 September. Left Jajno at 6:30 A.M. in the rain. Quite cold. Had to play en route. Covered approx 14 km, but not all that bad. Went through only one village, Huta Borowieńska, where played for the Germ. general as the troops filed past. Reached Otr. (bivouac), swampland, at 12:30. Had a five-course meal with Soukup, Gypsy-style, naturally. No sooner had we dug ourselves in than cannons from the nearby front started up. Nice weather, but oh my aching back: trudging through endless stretches of sand is no joke. Late in the afternoon we paid a visit to the cemetery, seven of our men and nine unknown Russians.

14 November. Nothing major since Thursday. One rehearsal after the other until the 11th, when we gave a concert for the Third Div. A 6-km march mostly on duckboards through endless marshes. The boards were narrow and covered with hoarfrost, so we kept falling. Played two masses and two violin concertos. Made tour of area, saw site of famous 4 April 1917 battle, bones still sticking up from ground. Set off for camp by candlelight along same duckboards. Awful march, didn't get back until midnight.

12 December. Left on leave.

1918

5 January. Back from leave, wonderful time, played in two churches. Had to go on to Dubnica, because regiment there again.

17 February. En route along Danube, Lower Austria. Coffee at Amstetten 9 A.M. An hour's stop. Wrote to Agi and to family. Fine weather. Mess at Osten San Florian. Bought wine, wrote to Agi. Evening coffee in Viedau.

20 February. Loaded trains in the morning and left for Trento. Trudged from one office to the next trying to find out where to go. Didn't find out until evening. Wrote to Agi and to Mama.

1 March. Left Grigno 10 A.M., marched through pouring rain to first It. town, Primubano. Stayed in Primubano until 5:30 P.M. Then marched up a very steep hill in the dark. Still raining, terrible march. Arrived at Erzego, approx. 1,000 meters above sea level, 10 P.M., dripping wet. Found an empty house, but had to nail a piece of tin over the window or, rather, what had been the window facing Italy. Froze without blankets, beds falling apart, left behind by fleeing population. Woken 3 A.M., grenade fire aimed at nearby road. Shivering with cold, lit fire in stove, but no chimney. Smoke poured out of windows and door.

4 April. Beautiful weather this morning. Italian aeroplanes circling overhead at noon. Watched battle between our air force and It. One plane lost its engine and glided down. Soukup got two food parcels. Cooked the grub.

14 June. Medals distributed. Waited for the offensive to begin in the evening. A beautiful night, everything still, but you could feel the storm ahead. The Italians started firing in the middle of the night, hoping to capture our *Feldwache.* Soon things quieted down again. At three we heard three shots fired one after the other like a clock striking the hour, following which the dark and still of night suddenly turned into the terrible flash and rumble of cannons coming together like a rush of raging water. I can't begin to describe the impression it made on me. I'd never experienced anything like it. And through it all I couldn't stop thinking of home and Mama and dearest Agi. The awful rumble went on nonstop until 8 A.M.

15 June. Until 8 A.M. our terrible cannonade and the Italians' return fire all jumbled together. We went out looking for horses—some to Porcelano, others to Grigno—but I was allowed to stay behind. I walked through the woods keeping an eye out for snow. The Italians kept up their fire nearby until 1. At 3 we had a telegram saying Col de Roso captured. The two naval cannons bombarding us now silent. Drizzles in the late morning, sky overcast, looks like we're in for a rainy spell. Fairly peaceful evening. Letter to Agička.

18 June. Terrible artillery fire all night, heavy shelling, the Italians again, until approx. 10. Pouring rain and thunder too. No letup at the front.

———

26 June. Played in Grigno for the men who fell in the most recent battles. Slightly queasy all day. Hadinec brought a letter from Anežka and two from Mama. Some artillery fire at the front.

1.4. In Czech the German word came out *orláb*. *Urlaub/orláb*—that is, "leave"—was usually granted for Christmas and for work in the fields, especially at harvest time. Father happened to be on agricultural leave at the end of August 1918. A leave tended to be two to three weeks long, and the soldier's local police station was informed of the date he was due back to make sure he did not overstay it. My father was under the surveillance of Police Chief Bělina. When his three weeks were up, however, he hid in the attic (my grandmother took him his meals), and there he stayed until the Czechoslovak Republic was declared on 28 October.

1.5. On the apex of the left lung, the size of a prewar Austrian five-crown coin.

2.1. The pig was slaughtered by Vilím Antoš, chief of the fire brigade. Before Father found a buyer for the Chomutičky house, which was made of wood and therefore insured against fire, Vilím advised him to "send the house to Fireborough" and actually proposed to do it for him "if you don't have it in you." Father rejected his kind offer and eventually sold the house for five thousand crowns to Splítek the gravedigger. It was torn down at the beginning of the Second World War, and all that remains of it is a small snapshot. I often saw Vilím dance at the firemen's balls and realized later that he was the spitting image of Gustave Doré's Don Quixote.

2.2. They bought up eggs, butter, and poultry in the villages surrounding Vysoké Veselí: Hradíštko, Žeretice, Volanice, Veležice, and Sběř, making the rounds on weekdays in a cart drawn by a mare named Bay (who was, oddly enough, black, but had a white patch on her forehead).

2.3. Grandmother went to market with the goods; Grandfather took over when she died. My grandparents were encouraged in their entrepreneurial endeavors by Grandmother's younger sister—Kousalová her married name was—who lived in Nový Bydžov and kept a stall at the local market. Grandmother's baskets were marked with the initials AV (Albína Vydrová). When we were children, we enjoyed playing with expired waybills, which were known as "avisos" at the time. We got them from a woman we called the "aviso lady," a thirty-five-year-old widow who would bring them from Ostroměř on her bike and whom Joska Řehák and Tonda Gabriel once saw in Obora Woods making love with a stranger in a railway uniform. Joska Řehák, the son of a gendarme officer who died soon after, started subscribing to *Národní právo* (National Rule), the organ of the Czech Fascist community, at the tender age of eighteen. Another Řehák, a wealthy peasant, became a Communist, though psychology rather than class origins accounted for his choice. He was a born naysayer: he opposed everything and everybody in the village. He refused to pay supplementary taxes for building a new school or straightening the riverbed; he refused to pay any taxes at all. One day he took a pitchfork to the tax collector. Tonda Gabriel was nicknamed Traveling Tonda because his father was a traveling salesman. There were three other Gabriels in the village: Josef and Václav, who were farmers, and Gabriel, a gardener. According to Grandfather, Chomutice had had seven Gabriels at the end of the century: Gabriel the Higher, Gabriel the Lower, Gabriel the Mason, Gabriel the German, Gabriel the Angel, Gabriel the Rabbit, and Gabriel the Pissed-Upon. Some moved away, others had no offspring.

3.1. While I was attending the K. V. Rais State Normal School in Jičín during the late thirties, I searched everywhere for him. He turned up of his own accord at the end of the Second World War. He was living on the outskirts of Prague and came begging to Father for food. Father sent him some smoked meat. He had a brother, an actor in Brno, I believe.

3.2. He used to single him out to the buglers. "Watch that little dark fellow when he plays. There's an embouchure for you!"

3.3. He told the whole story in a letter to his mother: "And then the bandmaster said to me: now I'd see who had more clout, him or the captain."

3.4. Father learned his German in Maffersdorf (now Vratislavice, just outside Liberec) in 1907 on the type of exchange visit common at the time. Hans Hlawatte, his counterpart in Chomutičky, called my grandmother "Mutti" and sent our family Christmas cards in German for thirty years, that is, until Munich. The cards invariably had bells with glass spangles on them.

3.5. Běchary, a village not far from Kopidlno, figures in the "The Devil and the Elf," a fragment from K. J. Erben's famous fairy-tale collection. The opening sentence reads: "Once upon a time there was a peasant who lived in Běchary and was known as Old Man Mallet."

3.6. The man in question was apparently August-Wilhelm (a.k.a. Auwi), a son of Wilhelm II. He was known for his close connection with the leaders of the NSDAP, the National Socialist German Workers Party.

4.1. To throw off enemy reconnaissance patrols, band members were detailed to the construction of fake tree-lined paths, which also served as roadblocks. Father brought home a pair of scissors designed to cut through barbed wire. The handle had an odd shape to it; it made me think of a bird of prey.

4.2. Father never got over the fact that instead of wearing their helmets (which his comrades in arms called "bomb hats") they had worked in their forage caps.

4.3. Since scores for marches and the repertory for military concerts and masses were readily available, Father spent most of his time copying out parts for the operettas the band was regularly called upon to play. His military diary contains the following notes: "Hung. Operetta Soc., Feb. 1916: 6th *Polenblut*, 8th *Zsuzsi kisasszony*, 12th *Rund um die Liebe*, 13th *Die ideale Gattin*, 15th *A kiskirály*, 19th *Rund um die Liebe*, 20th *Der Graf von Luxemburg*, 22nd *Die oder keine*, 26th *Zsuzsi kisasszony*, 27th *Rund um die Liebe*, 29th *Die oder keine*. March 1916: 2nd *Polenblut*, 4th *Tiszavirág*, 8th *Keverházi Konrád*," and so on until June. The performances were well attended by the officer elite and proceeded very much as Jaroslav Hašek describes them: "Lieutenant Lukáš . . . had left the camp and gone to the Hungarian theatre in Királyhida, where they were giving a Hungarian operetta. The leading roles were performed by buxom Jewish actresses, whose fabulous distinction was that when they danced they threw their legs up in the air and didn't wear either tights or drawers, and for the greater gratification of the officers they shaved themselves underneath like Tartar women. If the gallery got no gratification out of this, all the more fell to the share of the officers of the artillery, who were sitting down in the stalls and had taken with them to the theatre their artillery field glasses for this beautiful spectacle" (*The Good Soldier Švejk* [London: Penguin Books, 1974], p. 356).

5.1. After graduating from the School of Commerce at Hořice in the Krkonoše region, my Uncle Pepík went to work at the Smíchovský Printing Works in the Klárov district of Prague. (In 1945 a man by the name of Alvár Smíchovský was condemned by a Czech national tribunal for having maintained close ties with the Gestapo.) He liked to travel, and in 1910 visited Kyjov in Moravian Slovakia, where he had a picture taken of himself and a young lady wearing folk costumes. We had the picture in our album. He also brought his sisters presents: the chest for my mother, and for my Aunt Růženka, the third of the Vydra sisters (she died in the autumn of 1920, shortly after my birth, of consumption), a richly embroidered Kyjov folk costume. She apparently wore it often at patriotic and Sokol events.

5.2. Moravec, who was a watchmaker as well, kept shop in the arcade on Jičín's main square. He bought precious metals, and his schoolboy son was one of the best hockey players in the region. He gave me seventy-four crowns for the ring with the blue and white stone and sixty-two for the one with the heart-shaped ruby.

5.3. *Capári,* also called *kaufcvik,* is played with four cards and a maximum of five players. I played most often at the Budinas'. Mr. Budina was an upholsterer and had two sons, Joska and Arnošt. Karel Kalenský, the blacksmith's son, was also a regular. The two of us always lost because Mrs. Budinová would walk around the table, looking at the cards and kibitzing: "Pass, Oto, pass!" or "No, Arne! The king!" or "The jack, Joska, the jack—it's the only card you've got in that suit!" *Ferbl* was usually played for stakes of one to ten crowns. During the war I played at the Pateks' pub with the "gizzard gang," a group of butchers who bought and slaughtered diseased and dying cattle and sold the meat on the black market in Vrchlabí and other towns and villages up in the hills. The code word for the meat they thus obtained was "gizzard," hence their name. The members of the gizzard gang were rolling in money, whereas my friends and I were in rather straightened circumstances. We were often joined by the warrant officer of the gendarmerie, Sergeant Chytrý, whose wife, a Sudeten German, never quite mastered Czech and voted for Henlein's separatist party. In 1940 I fell in love with their daughter Arnoštka. Once, during the repression following Heydrich's assassination, the headwaiter won seven hundred crowns from Herbert Špigl and me in a game of twenty-one (the two of us played as one in what we called a "twin game"). He stuffed the banknotes into his pouch and poured each of us a jigger of cheap brandy. I had a job in Rychnov nad Kněžnou at the time and had to borrow the train fare from the owner. There were repercussions at home.

6.1. Koťátko was from Horní Kalná and came to Chomutice in 1930, during Father's term as mayor. He taught first at the primary school, then at the secondary school, and was active in the Sokol movement, the fire brigade, and the Freethinkers. He was quick to make friends with the local dignitaries, but was so aggressive that he later alienated some of them. He also directed a number of amateur theatricals and decorated the dance hall for festive occasions, reminding everyone he was the son of a professional decorator. He had two daughters and a wife who was in love with the local physician, Dr. Jandera. Dr. Jandera's elder sister used to receive love letters from the well-known painter Bohumil Kubišta. Whenever Koťátko's wife went for a checkup, she would undress before being called upon to do so. Owing to the doctor's lack of interest, however, the relationship remained platonic.

6.2. After the Jelínek scandal the authorities disbanded the local school board, replacing it with a single trustee. The first was a local brewer by the name of Kejř, the man who had leased the Obora brewery. His son Jiří, who later became a historian specializing in the reign of the Hussite king George of Poděbrady, was a friend of mine, and he and I would put on puppet plays at his house. Father was a frequent guest there as well, playing chamber music with Mrs. Kejřová, an excellent pianist, who performed at various local musicales and on special occasions like Christmas Eve. In the sixties, when the Catholic Church was all but destitute and could not afford musicians and when she herself was an elderly widow, she played the organ for all church services.

6.3. At the time, the mid-thirties, the Zet was the *dernier cri* in Chomutice. The only other person who had one was Rudolf Slatinka, the headmaster of the school, and he nearly demolished it taking my father for a spin one day. Father got off with a broken arm and a dislocated hip; Mr. Slatinka nearly lost his left eye.

6.4. The reason was that they were both so miserly. Their mother lived with the farmer brother, and the grocer brother didn't speak to her either, though he sometimes sent his daughter Mirča to see her. The farmer brother kept a boar and hung a sign saying "Pedigreed Rychnov Boar on the Premises" on the front of his house. The family was very religious. Josef Jr. regularly served as an acolyte, earning decent pocket money at weddings and funerals.

6.5. The girl was a Slovak from the Trenčin region. Slovak maids were quite common at the time, and it was all but a matter of course for the master have his way with them. Still, a certain discretion was called for, and sometimes the servant would wrap the master around her little finger. A servant girl by the name of Zuzka got her claws into an Obora farmer by the name of Jirák when his wife ran away with an official by the name of Koupil, a summer resident. Good Catholic that he was, he donated a plaster statue of Saint Theresa to the local convent of the Sisters of the Order of Saint Charles of Borromea to expiate his sin, and the Catholic children prayed to her, saying, "Tiny Theresa with soul pure as air, ask the child Jesus to grant us our prayer."

7.1. The office was opposite the shop, just across the road: It had a filing cabinet, a cupboard, a desk, and a typewriter. I was very much tempted to try my hand at the latter. The first time Jelínek invited me to the office, he explained how it worked and gave me a demonstration, the second time he allowed me to use it, and the third time he said things like, "What are you boys up to out there in the hay?" I was scared. I was afraid he'd tell Father. But he didn't give me time to answer. "Oh, it's nothing," he said, "we did it too when we were your age." And suddenly he came out with it: "What if *we* did it? You and me!" I didn't know where to turn. I was saved by old man Žďarský, who worked in the warehouse and suddenly stuck his head in to find out how much of the oats Mr. Jelínek wanted him to thresh. Žďarský was also the local gravedigger. His entire salary and everything he got for digging graves went for drink at Jelínek's shop. He had three daughters: Máňa, Tonča, and Fanda. Tonča had a longtime admirer in Joska Komárek, failed student, jack-of-all-trades, but mostly musician (singer and even, for a time after Mr. Valtera's departure, church organist), drinker, and gambler. When he finally married her in the mid-thirties, Monsignor Melich arranged for him to be made ticket clerk at the Chuchle railway station. He received about two thousand crowns from the Žďarskýs for setting up house, and old man Žďarský accompanied him to the station at Sobčice to make sure no harm came to him on the way. Komárek rode only as far as Ostroměř, one station down the line, then hurried back to the pub at Obora. He arrived just in time for a game of *ferbl* and lost the dowry down to the last crown. He was later dismissed from the Chuchle post for embezzlement.

7.2. A friend of mine studying auto mechanics in Hradec Králové. He was the son of Václav Stich, an egg and butter merchant, who had moved with his family to Chomutice in 1928. Mr. Stich sold his wares as far away as Tanvald, and in 1931 he brought back a German girl, Lea Hasta, to stay with his family for the summer. I was so taken with her that after she left in September I composed one of my first poems. It began in the following dreamy register: "It was summertime and thy face divine made me lose my mind. / Now my heart shall pine for its features fine though it ne'er be mine." Although it remained in manuscript form, the manuscript fell into the hands of a band of local scamps, who mocked my pining heart by shouting the first line over and over.

7.3. The son of František Fišera, the tailor my father was apprenticed to. He was a year older than I was. His father was over fifty when he was born. He would stand in front of confectioners' stalls at church fairs and pilgrimages, gawking hungrily at their wares, and take a fifty-heller coin out of his pocket, caress it with his eyes and fingers, look up at the sweetmeats again, and, utterly indifferent by then, slip the coin back into his pocket.

7.4. The son of a war invalid. He was apprenticed to an auto mechanic in Ostroměř and put together a motorcycle out of the parts of three wrecks: a Teroto, a Jawa, and a Praga. We called the result a Frantáz.

7.5. The son of the gendarmerie's warrant officer, who died in 1929. His mother was of German origin but spoke perfect Czech and stayed on in Obora with her son. During the occupation she refused to register as German. Herbert was in my class at school and later attended the School of Commerce at Hořice. He was handsome and a good athlete, and much as the Muses smiled upon me our flesh-and-blood local girls smiled upon him. He told me that during the night they spent in the hotel Jelínek wanted to share his bed, and when he, Herbert, threatened to make a scene he stretched his leg over Herbert's blanket and moaned, "Just let me leave my leg here. Just one leg." In the end he got hold of himself and crawled back under his covers.

7.6. Okrouhlický was a breeder of pedigreed goats. He had a son by the name of Jaroslav and an epileptic wife. People called him Cock Robin (presumably a reference to sodomy) or Natius (because he was baptized Hynek, that is, Ignatius). He went barefoot from spring to autumn and enjoyed spying on amorous couples, for which he received an occasional thrashing.

7.7. Bachelor, veteran of the Czech Legion in Russia, and longtime member of the Sokol Gymnastic Society Executive Board and District Council. Whenever the local amateur theater put on a patriotic work, he would play the Legionnaire.

7.8. Father had a black mustache all his life and never tired of twisting it. He even used a mustache trainer when I was small. He never shaved himself; he went twice a week to a barber by the name of Dušek, the husband of my Chomutice grandmother's younger sister and therefore his uncle. Until the end of the First World War Dušek had been a shopkeeper in the Hernals district of Vienna near Wurlitzergasse, the street where the shelter Adolf Hitler slept in was located.

8.1. We boys used it to make earphones and microphones. We would stretch it between cardboard circles and attach them with a long string or thread and make "telephone calls" with them. We had to shout if we wanted to be heard by the other party.

9.1. I didn't get the joke until I was eight. I started doing Sokol gymnastics at the age of six and attended my first Sokol event as a member of the Chomutice Section, Čižek-Jičín District. (I thought the Čižek part came from the song "Siskin, Siskin, Little Bird"—*čižek* being the Czech word for siskin—but I later learned it was the surname of a Sokol luminary.) It took place in Hořice in the Krkonoše Mountains. The district event—the Hořice event was local—was held in Rohoznice that year. I did not attend.

10.1. The news traveled fast and was the subject of heated discussion during feather-stripping sessions and hen parties. My paternal grandmother had the following to say about it: "Good Lord, that's rushing things, rushing things."

10.2. Operettas came quite late in the game. At first there were only plays with songs and dances: *The Šumava Beauty, Granddad's Fiddle,* or *Miller Švejnoha's Water Sprite.* The first operetta staged in Chomutice was patriotic in

theme; it was entitled *The Bugler Boy* and came to us from
Jára Kohout's theater in Prague. Its Chomutice debut took
place in 1937 at the Jiřičeks' pub. Jiřina Kozlová played the
daughter of a farmer named Patočka, who was played by a
merchant named Ruda Lobeč. Her love interest, Captain
Hodr of the Horse Marines, was played by my father, who
proved especially stirring in the arias "Youth, Golden
Youth" and "My Love's a Wondrous Thing, a Blue-Eyed
Princess Fair." The role of the colonel—"a military man
heart and soul," as the "Cast of Characters" had it—fell to
Cendelín the barber.

10.3. His abnormality made itself felt chiefly in bicycle
rides through the countryside, when he talked or sang to
himself. He had absolutely no interest in things sexual or
erotic and remained a bachelor. He was good-natured and
liked to give children rides on his bicycle.

10.4. After the death of Václav Antoš, former Czech Legionnaire in Italy and card shark. (Like Kazda the teacher,
he died of a brain tumor, and local gossips maintained it
came from the disease the two had contracted from the
same girl while in Italy.) But Kozel had had earlier experience with the post: until 1927 my father's predecessor was
a farmer by the name of Jireš, and Kozel served as his
deputy. As Jireš had other interests—he went hunting, traveled regularly to Bydžov as head of the Agrarian Party, raped
Slovak maids—Kozel in fact took charge of the "municipal
offices." He could do a perfect imitation of Jireš's signature
on residency permits and livestock health certificates.

10.5. The owner of the establishment specializing in
hard liquor was a man named Suchánek who had lost his
leg in the war. But a jolly old soul was he! He enjoyed
parodying the liturgy and singing old army songs. His pub
was a place of pilgrimage for all beggars and tramps passing
through Chomutice and the daily habitat of such denizens
of the poorhouse as Klapka, a.k.a. the Sardine, or of Huriga

Kykal, who slept in the Rajms' toolshed. Suchánek kept a wide-mouthed jar of rolls on the counter with "Crunchities" written on the label.

10.6. The investigation was initiated by Šimák the shoemaker, who became mayor after Kozel. During the proceedings it came out that a considerable sum had also been embezzled by a police agent named Horáček. Though the father of six children, Horáček did not spread his ill-gained wealth among them; like his superior, he spent it all on drink.

10.7. I had a tenuous connection with him. One day there were two pools of water in front of the Jiřičeks' pub, one small, the other a regular stream, and when Tonda Kunc asked Jiřiček how they got there he said, "Well, the Hiršal boy piddled and Tonda Tonar puddled."

11.1. The impulse for starting a Sokol chapter in Chomutice came from the Book Circle, which contributed a hundred crowns to the initial costs and provided the founding members in Mára, an estate manager, and Knob, a schoolmaster. Knob was elected head of the chapter; Fišera, a tailor, his deputy; Hojný, a teacher, gymnastics instructor; and Kulich, also a teacher, secretary. The first equipment—a bar, a sawhorse, a mat, and a few dumbbells—came entirely from donations. The sessions took place at the Komáreks' pub, which sported a portrait of the movement's founder, Miroslav Tyrš, with the motto "Muscles for the Motherland."

11.2. The concept and design were due entirely to Fišera the tailor, who had picked up quite a bit on his travels through Germany and Italy as an apprentice. He was the illegitimate child of a sugar executive of Jewish extraction. He was also, to use a word in vogue at the time, a madcap. For information about his son, see note 7.3.

12.1. She took active part in the activities until she was married; afterwards she was merely a contributing member. The songs she used to calm me down or put me to sleep—songs I have often found running through my unconscious, like "Raspberry Bush with Leaf So Broad," "Adam Had Full Seven Sons," "Siskin, Siskin, Little Bird," "Water Flowing, Water Ebbing," or "Down Fell My Sword from Black Stallion"—were all Sokol songs. The stallion song always made me cry, but I never stopped begging for it. Clearly an early manifestation of lyrical masochism.

12.2. "Fučík, Julius, Czech composer. Born Prague, 18 July 1872. After graduating from the Prague Conservatory and studying composition with Antonín Dvořák, he joined the symphony orchestra formed for the 1892 National Exposition and composed a wind trio, which enjoyed great success at the Czech Journalists Club. Since 1896 he has been a bandleader and choral director. After conducting the Croat choral society Danica for two years, he was appointed bandmaster for the Eighty-Sixth Regiment in Pest, where he is still active. Best known among his 260 works are the preludes (a variety of concert voluntary which he introduced); they include 'The March of the Gladiators,' 'Vive l'Empereur,' 'In Hussite Times,' etc. He has also composed two masses, an Ave Maria, the abovementioned trio for winds, thirty songs for male chorus, an orchestral suite (*Life*), four symphonic poems, a number of overtures, a violin method with piano and orchestral accompaniment, and *The Battle of Custozza* for the symphonic cycle *Honor and Glory to Austria*. Two choral works for men, 'Sjećaš li se još' [Do you still recall] and 'Zora sviće' [Dawn is breaking], are particularly popular in Croatia, as is the Slovene march 'Triglav' (Prague 1904)" (from *Ottův slovník naučný* [The Otto Encyclopedia], Volume XXVIII, Supplement, Prague, 1909). Father had a predilection for Julius Fučík, the marches and overtures in particular. He liked to play his "Dream Ideals" at dances, always announcing it as "Traumideale." Fučik died in Berlin in 1916 when Father was on furlough. Father is said to have taken the loss much to heart, and the members of his military band surely shared his sentiments. Julius Fučík was the uncle of the future "national hero" of the same name.

13.1. Litters had to be reported, but the reports were never verified. As a result, swine breeders could make a fortune. They usually traded their animals for agricultural products like wheat, potatoes, beets, straw, and hay. A piglet on the black market brought in more than a fattened hog at official prices.

13.2. Just such a runt must have been on Vladimír Holan's mind when he has the hero of his poem "Martin of Orel" say of a hog that refuses to leave the sty: "Clearly it's just a Heliogabal" (Vladimír Holan, *Příběhy* [Tales] [Prague: Československý spisovatel, 1963], p. 134).

13.3. The inspectors preferred smoked meat to fresh. The meat would be salted and then sit for six weeks in a vat (it was turned over only once, after the third week), whereupon it was smoked for two days over slowly burning prune-tree logs. Some of the home-smokers pickled the meat, that is, they added water to the vat and let the meat stand for, say, another three months. We found that disgusting. We smoked our meat at the municipal smoking chamber. Once the smoking process was over, we carved it into pieces and hung it to dry from a beam in the attic. A hog lasted nearly a year, until the time came to slaughter another. I couldn't resist going at it with my pocketknife on the sly. I left the fat and took only lean pieces. Even though I was given a sound thrashing each time, my innate gluttony continued to get the better of me.

14.1. Kozel had a handwriting very much his own, as thick, large, and round as the man himself. Every document written in his hand, even the simplest receipt, commanded respect. For a certain period Kozel also served as our local chronicler. When he was dismissed, however,

Karla Houžvičková, a teacher and member of the District Council, tore up many of the pages he had written. Unfortunately, they included the return of the Legionnaires in 1920.

14.2. When forced for pecuniary reasons to give up drinking, he would lose all control and become unreasonably vindictive. He was also caught stealing a quarter-kilo of butter.

15.1. They had had a run-in at the Bašnice railway station in 1924. They were on their way to see a Mr. Kubišta, sugar executive and owner of house number 7 in Chomutice, which he had put up for sale. Both men were interested in purchasing it. Šimák eventually yielded to Father because of his "seniority," and Father bought the house for twenty-five thousand crowns. (We had ten on hand and borrowed the rest from the Chomutice Agricultural Bank.) But there was always a certain tension between them. Šimák was very ambitious and envious of Father's position as mayor. He calmed down a bit when he took over as mayor, and showed Father a certain respect. He plied his cobbler's trade in a tiny wooden house with one apprentice and one journeyman, yet dreamed of competing with the great magnate Baťa. For a time he sold his wares under the brand name Bussi and even came up with an advertising slogan: Bussi Shoes for Busy Feet. Whenever I had my shoes resoled or their tips reinforced, I enjoyed watching the shoemakers work and listening to their stories and political discussions.

15.2. Owing to the solidarity of certain officials in the Protectorate imposed by the Germans in 1939, the tables were often turned on Czechs who denounced their fellow Czechs. Corruption was also a major factor. Even the Germans could be bribed. A woman named Papoušková who lived off her private income in the nearby village of Staré Smrkovice smoothed over an anti-Nazi remark by donating a side of pork to the Gestapo and even managed to get someone out of a concentration camp for a whole animal.

16.1. As I have mentioned before, Father served as Fišera's apprentice. He had previously been apprenticed to a gardener in Lázně Bělohrad, but the work was arduous and Bělohrad too far from home, and he ran away after six weeks or so. It was then that Grandmother decided to apprentice him to a tailor.

16.2. Father wrote Mother approximately five hundred letters, not counting picture postcards (reproductions of artworks for the most part, though photographs of the front as well). Mother wrote less often: her letters come to about three hundred plus a hundred postcards. My daughter Kristina has Father's letters with her in Vienna; nearly all Mother's correspondence has been lost. One day I came across two letters in Chomutice. I reproduce them here in their entirety.

In the field, 10 June 1917

Dear Agička,

Sunday morning again, the time when I used to stop and see you after Mass, I always enjoyed watching you bustle about in the kitchen, sometimes I came home spotted with flour. Remember how we'd plan our afternoon walks? You can't imagine how I miss those times, I can't get them out of my mind. How I looked forward to those Sundays and now I wish they wouldn't come at all. Every Sunday we play for Mass and give an afternoon concert. Today we go all the way from four to eight, it's for the reserves, near the front, and I can hear a little shooting again today. Time for mess so I'll stop here, more later . . . Later in the afternoon. I'm glad you got my letter from K, sweetheart, I've sent you another one since, just as long. Many thanks for your letter from the 3rd and 4th, I wish every letter you wrote was as long. Soukup thanks you for your greetings and returns them and sends greetings to Mařka and hopes she will be lucky in love. When I come home on leave they'll have to give us our bench back, I can't imagine it won't be empty at least some of the time. I can't wait to get on that train, sweetheart. You say you'd like to see our under-wear, would you be surprised! Actually, you can go to our house and see it, I sent my winter underwear home, I wore it for nearly six weeks and it's white as paper. When I get home I'll show you how we wash it without soap or soda, it takes half the day. We're washing again tomorrow, I can't say as I'm looking forward to it. This whole war is full of things like that, there's nothing to hope for . . . Remember the afternoon we spent at the Vondráčeks' two years ago, my last Sunday as a civilian? Remember what a nice time we had except for that one weak moment, though it wasn't that bad, was it? If I could visit you today, we'd have an even better time. I keep dreaming of seeing you again, sweet-heart, I longed for you when I was in Sopron too, believe me, but that was nothing compared with the way I feel now. Every night Soukup and me talk about the good times we're going to have, I wish you could hear what we've got planned. He keeps telling me you don't really have fun together until you tie the knot and I won't know what he means till we're man and wife. Anyway, I'll tell you everything when I get home, I hope you like it. I can't finish my letter today because after mess I lay down and slept until two. You'll forgive me if I wait till morning, won't you, sweetheart? I have to go and play now . . . Last night I sent you a card at least and now I'll finish this letter. There were rumors today of a move to the Tyrolean hills, which would not make me happy. I'll let you know when I hear more. One of our aeroplanes is flying overhead and the Russkies are shooting at it but keep missing. We've got two weeks of clean clothes now, it took us a whole half-day and we were soaked by the end of it, but you should see how white the underwear is! . . . Don't forget to say hello to the family from time to time, Mama's always happy when you drop in, she was thrilled you stayed the whole afternoon last time. I sent Bohouš Uxový congratulations on his wedding, a little early maybe. I miss you, Agička, but that's life, the most I can hope for is that I'll come back safe and sound and we'll soon be man and wife forever. Give everybody my regards, sweetheart, and congratulate Dad if things went his way at the recruitment office. I shower you with ardent kisses and heartfelt greetings!!!

Yours,
Pepouš

Dear Pepouš,

You're not mad at me for not writing on Sunday, are you? There were all kinds of things I meant to write, believe me, I'm always thinking of things I want to write, but when the paper's in front of me and the pen is in my hand I can't do it, I haven't got a thought in my head. So I just sit there, my mind wandering here, there, and everywhere, thinking of one thing and another and what things will be like eventually, but most of all I think of you, Pepouš, and the coming Christmas. You know how much I'm looking forward to it, Pepouš, because I write about it in every letter. You will come, won't you? I don't want to be disappointed the way I was last time. Christmas would lose all its charm for me. For the time being I'm thinking only as far as the holidays, not beyond. Thank you so much for the card dated the 14th, it came today, but the letter you mention in it hasn't come yet. The same holds for your letter of the 2nd, which leads me to believe it won't come at all. Where could it be I wonder? I've got some stationery ready for you, I'll enclose it in tomorrow's letter. You have enough for now, haven't you? I couldn't get any more into the envelope. They're requisitioning again for the army, they're really rushing it this year, and what will be left for spring? They should at least have waited for the harvest to be in. It was five weeks ago today we had our sad evening, time does fly, but I can't forget . . . If only peace was in sight, but no, things are still the same, worse if anything. We did so hope in Russia, and now they're fighting among themselves. If they'd had their wits about them, the war wouldn't have lasted a year, and now they're dragging it out something awful. Though what good does it do to follow things, it's better to forget all about it . . . I hope your letter gets here tomorrow. Can you tell me when you think you'll be coming? I promise to write before Sunday, but that's it for today. I'm looking forward to seeing you soon and send you an ardent hug.

Yours,
Anežka

P.S. Regards from everybody!

16.3. Later in life Mother rarely went to Prague. During the last visit before her illness—she died of cancer in 1978—

she expressed a desire to cross the bridge that had been built across the Nusle Valley. It had been a childhood dream of hers.

17.1. A disease common among men who work with sandstone or in quarries. It is caused by inhaling silicon dust.

17.2. She never knew her father. He is said to have been a deserter making his way through the countryside, though according to Grandmother he was a young worker from the quarry at Vojice who was killed by a falling rock before she was born and before he could marry her mother.

17.3. My great-grandmother was disowned by her family and thrown out of the house before the child was born. She was delivered in a manger like the Virgin Mary. She tried hiring herself out as a seasonal worker, but had trouble finding employment with a babe in arms.

17.4. Vacek, the schoolmaster there, took her in, and she lived with his family until she finished school.

17.5. Grandmother enjoyed talking about Jewish rituals: the kosher butchering, the prayers, the celebration of the sabbath and other holidays she experienced at the Kháns'. She always spoke of her masters with respect, but maintained a certain Catholic distance and, though tolerant (like her employers), claimed that if a Gentile went out with a Jewess "the girls would tear him limb from limb." I can report from personal experience that she was mistaken.

17.6. Grandfather's first wife died of tuberculosis at the age of twenty-two. She was buried in the old cemetery next to the parish house, which we called the churchyard or *Kirchhof*. No one was buried there after 1901, when a new cemetery was begun just outside the village.

18.1. In the small wooden house Grandfather had there. See notes 24 and 25.

18.2. Most of them are gone now, replaced by monuments of artificial stone, a combination of cement and gravel. They used to be found not only in the Chomutice cemetery but in cemeteries for miles around. According to Mother, they were particularly numerous in Veležice, where she would go with her parents for butter and eggs.

18.3. When the dance he was playing for was over, the innkeeper would let him sleep on a table. The next morning he would be given a drink before he set out for other pubs. His favorite was a weak brew made of rye and known as "mason's" or "pure" brandy. He would down a quarter of a liter at a time.

18.4. I heard about his perigrinations from Uncle Pepík, who took violin lessons from him. After having his pupils play the exercises he had assigned, he would laud or excoriate them depending on his mood and either assign the next exercise or reassign the last one. Few of his pupils became musicians. The more gifted and assiduous among them also took lessons on a wind instrument. He himself played the violin and the bass flugelhorn.

18.5. Grandfather does not appear to have been particularly happy in his second marriage. For a time the newlyweds had my great-grandmother living with them, and since after her personal tragedy she had every reason to hate men, she may have infected her daughter with her feelings. In any case, he started hitting the bottle.

18.6. She would go from pub to pub. "Hiršal the music man? Right. The day before yesterday, just before lunch. He said he was going to the Kubíns' pub in Noreturn. That means the Macheks' in Bonfire is next. Which would put him in Big Yucksville at the Bydžovskýs' about now." Grandfather tempered his sprees with snuff. He was a nonsmoker.

18.7. He drank while he worked as well. He had the stone for the central monument in the new Chomutice cemetery delivered to the courtyard of the Antošes' pub under the pretext that there wouldn't have been room enough at home. The monument is still standing. It consists of a Christ on the cross and the following verse:

> O earth, dear earth, the end to worldly fame!
> On earth we are diverse, but in the earth the same.
> We slumber till we hear the trumpet's call.
> The Judgment Day awaits us one and all.
> But now we sleep secure for Christ our Lord
> Hath consecrated with His death this sward.
> So grant us everlasting life,
> Blissful, peaceful, free of strife.

"Václav Hiršal, A.D. 1901" is engraved on the back.

19.1. Grandmother very much identified with her son, my father. An 1898 photograph of my grandfather with his two sons (Grandmother refused to be included because Grandfather had been out on one of his sprees) shows Father in a velvet dress with large buttons and shoes coming up to his calves, while Uncle Václav had on long twill trousers and a corduroy jacket going down to his knees.

19.2. After my uncle finished school, Grandfather wanted to teach him the trade himself, but he ran away several times. Each time it took three days to find him.

19.3. As long as he was a cowan (which was what unskilled masons were called), he did little more than stir, that is, mix the mortar, but he eventually entered masonic nobility and worked exclusively on facades.

19.4. The Antoš family owned a large estate as well. See note 37. The publican's name was František, and he had a brother whose name was Václav. The latter attended the School of Sculpture in Hořice and studied under the well-known Myslbek at the Academy in Prague. He became quite well known himself and spent part of his professional life in Russia. It was he who sculpted the Christ on the cross of the monument Grandfather made for the Chomutice cemetery. See note 18.7.

19.5. It amounted to two hundred gulden, which Grandmother had to borrow from the bank at Hořice.

20.1. The address in Father's war notebook is Václav Hiršal, Prisoner of War, Kamenskoe, Zaporozhye, Yekaterinskaya gub, Dnepr Factory, House No. 473. He also gives Uncle Pepík's address: Josef Vydra, Austrian Prisoner of War, Mako Chervonnots, Velinskaya gub, Moskovskaya-ekon. Rossia.

20.2. This did not come to light until my uncle's funeral, when a teacher named Křížek told the whole story of his Legionnaire past—to no credit of the deceased, I must say. He called Uncle Pepík a bad soldier, a man whose hatred for the Emperor led him to shirk his military obligations. He described his attempt to make Uncle Pepík join the Legion and Uncle Pepík's hesitation until the Legion's victory at Zborov. He went on to call Masaryk the champion of the nation's future, spoke of Julius Fučík in the same vein, and ended by saying that Uncle Pepík had always been a loyal citizen of the Republic.

21.1. Besides the gun from Russia we had two *Handgranaten* my father had brought home from the war. They looked like goose eggs. For a while he kept them under Grandmother's trousseau chest and we played with them when we were young, but eventually he got rid of them. Then there was Father's revolver, which lay fully loaded on his bedside table in the big room. I was always afraid he was going to shoot me one day. During the Occupation he buried the gun and removed the revolver as well, but in such a way as to be able to retrieve it easily: he stashed it behind a beam in the attic, where it remained until the war was over. In May 1945 he brought it down and used it to help capture the column of Nazi tanks that happened to be in Chomutice. Thanks to his knowledge of German he was able to mediate between the local patriots and the tank commander. The latter was willing to surrender, but only to someone in uniform. Luckily, the rebels recalled that a retired tax inspector by the name of Jór was living in Chomutice, and he pulled out his moth-eaten uniform from his wardrobe and took the Germans prisoners. The next day the Red Army marched in and relieved us of them.

21.2. As such he was highly admired and esteemed, at least during the immediate postwar years. But even later— for national holidays like the commemoration of Hus's martyrdom on 7 July or the founding of the Republic on 28 October, or to celebrate the ritual plantings of our Czech linden tree, the opening of a school, and the like— his uniform commanded respect. Besides, the Legionnaires Bank granted him an interest-free loan to build a new barn and stable.

22.1. Grandmother never brought up her relations with the prisoners. Her love life after Grandfather's death was a closed book. All we know is what Mother let fall shortly before her death, namely, that in 1908 she had had the banns read twice in church (why the all-important third reading never took place is a mystery) and was supposed to marry Růžička the barber, who had spent twenty-five years in the Valdice prison for the murder of his beloved, Máňa Kyselková. He got her pregnant, as the story goes, and then, aided by an accomplice, hanged her. Why the marriage failed to materialize I never discovered. Grandmother had another admirer in the twenties in the person of a widowed farmer neighbor and notorious drunk by the name of Záveský. Nothing came of it. When as children we saw him staggering along the street in his cups, we would cry out, "Cholera! Cholera!" and sing the following ditty:

> If you're feeling choleric,
> You may need to shit a brick.
> What's the best thing you can do?
> Find the nearest loo!

23.1. Old lady Laloušková had a bachelor beau whose name was Jágl and who had been blind since the turn of the century. He called his companion "my little housekeeper," played the accordion, and gave political speeches. He claimed to be a "Marxist Communist" and dictated his ideas and reflections to a schoolboy, who also read the Communist daily *Rudé právo* (Red Rule) and various Marxist tracts aloud to him. He kept a diary, each entry of which began: "Workers of the world, unite!" His ideas and reflections had a certain impact, and my father often dropped in and chewed the fat with him. Only Rýgl the landowner couldn't stand him. Once he went and told him point-blank, "Why keep going on about things you can't see!"

23.2. While I was studying at the normal school in Jičín, they took in a relative, a girl studying at the school of commerce in Hořice. We boys all called her Snazzy. I once took her to a dance, and when I tried to kiss her good-night at the pond she pushed me away with the words, "Why should I kiss a stranger?" Six months later she was dating a young man from Vojice, and the boys told me they'd seen them down by the Javorka doing it together.

24.1. See note 18.1.

25.1. Grandmother was very religious. She taught me to say the Lord's Prayer, Hail Mary, My Guardian Angel, and the Angelus before bed. When stirring dough she never forgot to make three crosses over the kneading trough with the stirrer, and before climbing into bed she would cross herself and say, "The Lord of Hosts goes first and I, sweet Mother of God, do follow." Misconstruing the formula, I asked her once, "How do you all fit in the same bed?"

25.2. Maximilián also moved the stove for us when we moved to Chomutice. While dismantling it, he released a swarm of black cockroaches.

26.1. Many years later I saw a similar one in the Smetana Museum. It was the piano on which Smetana composed *The Bartered Bride*. Ours lacked the reinforced sounding board, but it had the same ivory and ebony keys, it was the same shape, and the music rest had the same design carved into it.

26.2. At the musicals and Sokol events the program was classical. Father would sing arias from operas by Smetana, Dvořák, and Blodek, for instance, "Could I But Wash Away My Guilt," "When Zdeněk Mine," "True Loves" (which he sang with Mrs. Jeriová from Sobčice), "We Wandered through Foreign Lands" (ditto). The high point of the evening was always the Blodek aria "Thou dearest, dearest Veruna." New Year's called for a lighter, cabaretlike repertory. Anda Kulichová would sing "There Once Was a Little Dutchman," Jiřina Kozlová "Granny, What a Wind!" and Fanda Žďarská "When Fate Chains a Lass to Poverty." The New Year's program was designed by the firemen themselves. Fire Chief Jireš would come out with a drum bouncing on a pillow-paunch and sing:

> Rat-tat-tat, Rat-tat-tay,
> When the drums begin to play,
> Rat-tat-tat, Rat-tat-tance,
> The boys no longer dance.

Then his deputy chief, Mayor Antoš, dressed in an apron, would iron and sing:

> I am a servant girl fair,
> My mistress a witch hard to bear . . .

26.3. I was particularly moved by "Remember the Days" (from *The Good Old Days,* a musical tableau by Jiří Červený) as sung by Father and Bohuša Slatinková, the head-master's daughter, who eventually married an engineer by the name of Václav Dašek and joined the well-known Hlahol Choral Society in Prague. She once invited Father to a rehearsal and introduced him to the soloist Eva Žitná (later Beránková). Every time he went to Prague, the Dašeks would take him to the opera at the National Theater. He always brought the programs home. Most of the operas were Czech classics, but he went to *Carmen* and *Tannhäuser* as well. Nor did they scorn an occasional operetta.

27.1. He would buy the song for 1.80 crowns and write out the parts himself. It was much cheaper than the arrangement, which would have run him sixteen crowns.

27.2. I could make little more of the title than a musty smell.

27.3. The small sandstone monument bears the inscription *Here Lies Pepíček Javůrek. Rest in Piece, Dear Child.* As a boy I was incensed at the elementary spelling error both here and in a Sobčice sign that read *Sold by the Peace.*

29.1. The flugelhorn and the trumpet were made by a Hradec Králové firm called Červený, the violin by František Kolář of Brtev near Lázně Bělohrad. Kolář was originally a peasant and did not come to violin-making until at a dance one night he sat on a musician's instrument and put it back together himself. The novelist Karel Václav Rais wrote a story about him, dubbing him Nogrief. Kolář also made a violin for the concertmaster of the National Theater with the odd-sounding name of Buchtele. Father often went to Brtev to buy instruments for his pupils, and once he took me and my brother Mirek along. On the trip Kolář promised to make me a cello when I was big enough for it. He also lent Father an unusual instrument of his own making: a violin whose soundboard consisted of small chips of burnt wood, like matches, and whose back and ribs were made of maple decorated with a floral pattern. The violin had a pleasing voice, and Father played it for three years to mellow it further. Shortly thereafter Kolář fell off a hay wagon and was killed. We also had Grandfather's violin.

See note 35.1 below. It had a beautiful dark finish, but for a long time could not be played because the soundboard was cracked, Grandfather having whacked Horák, the violist, over the head with it during a concert. When I entered the normal school, Father had it repaired and refinished in a lighter shade by the Jičín violin maker Patočka. It then became mine. It had a slightly weaker voice than Father's. Although it bore no marks of identification, Patočka thought it possibly the work of one Věnceslav Metelka, a self-taught violin maker and the model for Čižek the schoolmaster in Rais's novel *Provincial Patriots.*

29.2. In 1931 the band members voted to remove Bílek the carpenter from his post as bandmaster—he was too old—and to put Father in his place. Zmatlík and Klapka were entrusted with the task of breaking the news to him. They came to our house before and after, before to consult on the procedure and after to report on the outcome. It went off without a hitch. Bílek's wife said, "I always said it would end like this," and Bílek wasn't particularly con-cerned about the loss in revenue. There was no one in the family to succeed him. True, he had a son—Josef was his name—but the son had a tin ear; he wasn't much of a carpenter either. By the time our paths crossed he was forty and a confirmed bachelor, though people said that when he was young he would walk girls home from the pub through the willow grove and tempt them with the line, "How about a little roll in the hay, baby!" Anyway, my father took over the band, and beside the red plaque with the dual-headed Bohemian lion and the words "Town Council" on it a small sign appeared on the front of the house, reading: Josef Hiršál, Bandmaster. It took a good dose of enamel to white out the accent over the *a,* which later turned up repeatedly in class registers.

29.3. Josef Haken comes up in *From My Life,* the mem-oirs of the poet Vítězslav Nezval. Head of the Communist Party until 1929, when he was succeeded by Gottwald,

Haken enjoyed a certain notoriety among the public at large. Like Olda Líman, my fellow student at the Jičín normal school, he came from Markvartice. Olda Líman enjoyed no notoriety. Father would speak of Haken with respect, adding, however, that he tended to be too radical. The cleaning lady who worked for him while he taught at Třtěnice was of quite a different opinion. "His poor wife!" she confided in my grandmother, who then passed it on during feather-stripping sessions. "The grief he put her through! Making passes left and right, drinking like a fish. And the mouth he had on him!"

29.4. The program consisted primarily of antiwar but pro-Czech songs like "Hold Me, Mother, in Your Arms," "Gone for a Soldier, Still But a Child," "Dragged Off To Serve," "Mother Dear, Father Dear," and so on. Father claimed that Haken put some of Fráňa Šrámek's anarchist, antimilitarist poems to music.

30.1. There was a small river, the Lužanka, flowing nearby. It was lined with reeds and teeming with schools of small fish: bream, bleak, tench, roach. The older boys caught them with rods or their hands. Tonda Záveský once gave me a tiny bleak in a Kalla herring tin. I cried for two days when it died.

30.2. Near Pond Field, just above a ditch on the Antošes' land, there was a wayside cross made by my Grandfather Václav. It was engraved with the following text: "Hail to Thee a Thousand Times, O Most Holy Christ! Erected at the Expense of the Antoš Family of Malé Chomutice. Václav Hiršal fecit."

30.3. Next to Kabáty Field there was a row of Bosnian pear trees. When I was very young, we would take them to the Šustrs to be dried. They were laid out on trays, and as soon as the sun started baking them they would give off a tempting fragrance. We called them sun-baked. The older boys would sneak into the drying room and steal them.

Rumor had it that twelve-year-old Joska Šustr and Pepka Veselá indulged in impure activities in the attic above the drying room.

30.4. It was so far away that a team of cows took two hours to get there. But in autumn I could gather a bumper crop of mushrooms—even orange and yellow boletuses—in no time flat.

30.5. Part of the feast was a mass held in the chapel. The congregation sang the following hymn:

> Mother of Mary, Most Holy Saint Anne,
> Be my protector in all that you can.
> Torments may plague me, I will not yield.
> Mother of Mary, my hope and my shield.

The Czechoslovak Church held its own service under the linden tree behind the chapel, and its congregation sang "Hus Burned at the Stake":

> Behold, O God of love,
> These Czech arms raised to Thee.
> Like Thee we sacrificed our son,
> Pledge of eternity.

The feast also featured booths with toys, sweets, and pickled cucumbers. After mass Father's band led a procession from the chapel to the Holces' pub, where there was a dance.

31.1. Baron Liebig had acquired the estate of Obora upon marrying the daughter of its owner, Raimund Ritter von Blaschke. The baron was known as a pioneer in the use of the motor car, and no one would have dreamed of missing the spectacle when before the Great War he and his family would arrive in three roadsters for a brief visit.

31.2. At first Horák's family—his widow and three sons— lived most of the year in Prague, leaving the estate in the care of a steward and his assistant. Later, however, Madame

Nina took over the reins. The tenant farmers and seasonal laborers referred to her as "Horačka" or "the owner" among themselves. In 1930, when the Depression was beginning to make itself felt, they resolved to wrest the estate from the hands of their exploiters, but got only so far as appointing the postrevolutionary leaders: Huňková the milkmaid was to be the assistant steward, Žolka the cheesemaker the steward, and Šulc, the coachman and father of five, the owner.

31.3. He was a powerful, swarthy man who looked like a Romanian. He opposed the construction of a new school because he was the biggest taxpayer in the school district. The laborers on his estate lived three families to a room with only a rope to separate them. They slept on bunks infested with bedbugs and fleas. Somewhere along the line he had himself appointed mayor, and when the district received emergency funds after a devastating hailstorm he kept the money. See note 23.1.

32.1. All we had to do was raise our voices or drop something and the door to the tiny room or main room would fly open and out would bound Father in his lace-up long johns, raring to give us a spanking. As his mother put it, Father was "hot-tempered."

33.1. "Moor, Karel. Czech composer. Born Lázně Bělohrad, 1873. He began his career as a secondary-school teacher and has also conducted various theater orchestras. He is the author of an oratorio (*Moses*), a one-act *féerie* (*Viy*), three full-length operas (*Hjördis, William Ratcliffe,* and *The Wise Fool*), a number of symphonic poems (*Polonia, The Sea, Requiem, Life, Unceasing Grief Within My Soul Doth Dwell*), quartets, songs, operettas (*A Schoolmaster in Hell,* etc.), piano pieces ('The Loner's Lament'), and an autobiographical novel (*Karel Martens,* 1904–5)" (from *Masarykův slovník naučný* [The Masaryk Encyclopedia], Volume IV [Prague, 1929], p. 1034). Karel Moor died in

1945. Father was introduced to him late in the thirties at Lázně Bělohrad's Pheasant Grove by a bandmaster named Rulf. One of their topics of conversation was the composer's son, who was about to enter the Vienna Conservatory. Many years later I met the composer's daughter, the actress Pavla Maršálková (née Moorová).

33.2. At one Pheasant Grove concert Father had finished the flugelhorn solo for "Lost in a Wood" (I don't know the name of the composer) in a clump of bushes far from the orchestra when someone gave him a poke in the ribs and asked, "Hey, what regiment were you with?" It was Captain Mach. A number of Father's pupils were accepted at the Military Music School as a result of this encounter. Captain Mach introduced Father to the head of military bands, Colonel Prokop Oberthor, at a concert conducted by the latter. The band that played was made up of a thousand members. "What do you say to that?" he asked Father, and Father said it sounded like a gigantic organ.

33.3. After his funeral Father received the following letter from Karel Vacek:

28 August 1942

Dear Friend,

I shall always be grateful for the incomparable devotion with which you participated in my dear father's funeral. The music you played and sang and the speech you made over the grave displayed great humanity. Unworthy tribute that these modest thanks may be, please accept them from all of us who so prized your willingness to comfort us in our hour of need.

Yours most faithfully,
Karel Vacek

34.1. "Kramolín, Josef. Czech painter. Born Nymburk, 1730; died Karlsbad, c. 1801. He received his elementary education in his native Nymburk, then studied painting and, in 1758, entered the Jesuit Order as a lay brother. Active as an artist in the Order until its abolition, he later worked at the Cistercian Monastery in Osijek, where he decorated the chapter room with frescoes depicting the history of the Order and the monastery itself. He spent the last years of his life in Karlsbad. The best known of his many works include: *The Apotheosis of Saint Bartholomew* (above the main altar at Saint Bartholomew's in Kolín, signed Jos. Kramolín pincxit Carloth. 1801), the Saint Barbara altar in the same church, the frescoes for Saint John's in Týnec nad Labem (dated 1781 but destroyed by fire in 1834) and for the churches in Třebechovice (dated 1780) and Štětí (dated 1785), and the Saint Wenceslas altar and frescoes for the church in Mikulovice near Chrudim" (from *Ottův slovník naučný* [The Otto Encyclopedia], Volume XV [Prague, 1900], p. 651).

35.1. At one point the two exchanged violins. Hlavsa's violin was better—it had a richer tone. See note 29.1. He gave it to Grandfather so it could be heard at the dances where he played. Father Hlavsa dreamed of uniting Chomutice, Chomutičky (or Malé Chomutice, as it was officially called at the time), and Obory (formerly Radeč, the seat of the Radecký family, from which, according to Palacký, the famous Marshal Radetzky was descended). Hlavsa proposed that the town thus formed be named František Josef, that is, Franz Joseph. The proposal was not adopted.

35.2. As children we all greeted him with the words "Praised be Our Lord Jesus Christ!" regardless of our religious background. His response was always a polite "Praised be He forever and ever!" One day Joska Budina ran behind a fence after he had passed, and called out, "White collar! Black ass!" The priest never turned a hair. Before the Budinas moved to the building of the old school, which they bought in 1933, they lived next door to us. See note 5.3. The house had a sign that said "Otakar Budina, Saddler and Upholsterer." We made it into an incantation that went "Rakato anidub relddas dna reretslohpu." We loved shouting it, especially while playing cops and robbers: it became the formula we used to arrest the culprit.

35.3. It consisted of a thick white porridge leavened with yeast and eaten together with a boiled potato. It was often served seven days in a row, which meant it was reheated and rebuttered seven times over.

36.1. See note 39.

36.2. The Free Thinking Movement came to Chomutice in the mid-twenties. Its members wore pins in their buttonholes (in the form of a pansy), paid dues, and subscribed to a magazine entitled *Havlíček* (for the martyr-journalist's pro-Czech or anticlerical stance) and peddled by Houžvičková herself. She was an old-maid schoolteacher who lived with her mother, the headmistress, in a beautiful wooden house with two linden trees in front of the windows. She was a passionate atheist and a fine figure of a woman. The issue of her virginity was the subject of much conjecture and as many regrets. Old man Vaníček, who built her a well, had this to say, for example: "There I was down in the well, and what do I look up to see but the young lady without her panties. Well, I'd never seen the likes of it, let me tell you: big as a bonnet and black as velvet."

36.3. She gave me a low mark in conduct when I was eight, supposedly for having set fire to a wreath at the cemetery on All Souls' Day, but actually for having a father involved in church music activities. True, I did set fire to the wreath, but I didn't mean to. It lay on Father Hlavsa's grave and had wax flowerets and, in the middle, an oil lamp with a burning wick. When I tried to use the wick to light a homemade candle whose own wick was too long, the flame flared up and grazed one of the wax flowers and the whole wreath caught fire. Everyone in the cemetery came running—including Žďárský the gravedigger with his shovel in tow—and formed a procession to take me home. An advance guard of two heralds preceded us, so Father was waiting at the gate with a large wooden spoon behind his back. Two women, Bejrová and Kejzlarová, had me each by an ear. Father performed the thrashing *coram publico.* The next day in school Houžvičková had a go at me as well, and to top it all off I was bawled out by Mr. Slatinka, the headmaster. Even though the latter told Father at a Sokol meeting that he considered the affair closed, Houžvičková used it as a basis for the low mark. Father, knowing full well the reason for it, gave me another thrashing and refused to sign the report. Mother had to forge his signature in the proper box.

37.1. See note 19.4. Antoš's daughter sang in the choir on Sunday morning and went out with the organist in the afternoon. Some of the boys would spy on them, and they reported that for a believing Catholic and a little man with a soft voice and a head shyly cocked the organist was rather enterprising *in eroticis.* Planning as he was to build a house-cum-shop in the vicinity of the school then under construction, he decided to combine *utile cum dulci* and bank on a dowry.

37.2. He gave my brother and me several picture books when in 1927 or thereabouts Father refused payment for singing with him at a funeral. They included *Czech Tales and Legends* by Josef Kalenský (I was fascinated by the fairy tale "Vaňura, the Devil's Helper") and *Tom Thumb's Alphabet Book,* an interesting attempt to teach the letters of the alphabet using poems and illustrations. I can still recite some of the poems, though I don't recall the authors' names.

38.1. Father cleaned his instruments after each playing with a product called Sidol. I haven't seen it in the shops for ages. It's probably no longer made.

39.1. His conversion was very hard on Grandmother, especially as he took the whole family with him. When she learned that each member received an identity card and had to pay the kind of dues you pay to the Sokol or the fire brigade, Grandmother was certain we would roast in Hell. She crossed herself in horror one day when I went off to take communion administered by Deacon Bohumil Lufinka in a Vysoké Veselí pub called At the Top. Even though the religious instruction class of the Czechoslovak Church was more like recreation than catechism, Deacon (later Father) Lufinka noted "Disobedient Devil" next to my name, and since his remark was unfortunately not unique I again received a low mark for conduct.

39.2. Though when, in 1951, he was dying of cancer he would clasp his hands and recite the Lord's Prayer and Hail Mary.

39.3. Father had no sympathy for the Baroque litany. He was a typical romantic and—his choleric temperament notwithstanding—lyrically inclined. You could feel it in the way he sang and played the flugelhorn. He was not interested in counterpoint; he felt at home with melody only.

40.1. He would come to Chomutice two or three times a year to visit his parents and sister. Once, when he was due and I wanted to go with Grandpa to meet him, Mother told me to wash my hands. I apparently refused, saying, "What if he doesn't come?" My other two uncles were generous too and never forgot their sister's progeny. Uncle Ruda, a teacher, gave us our first children's books: *Fairy Tales,* illustrated by Aleš and told by Václav Říha; Eliška Krásnohorská's *Tale of the Wind; Berona, Bolenka,* and *Lidka* in the "white book" series with illustrations by Artuš Scheiner. In 1933 I found skis under the Christmas tree from him, one of which I managed to break the very next day (Mr. Kosina, the local wheelwright, eventually made me a replacement). Uncle Ruda sent me useful books when I was studying at the normal school, books like Vítězslav Nezval's *Modern Trends in Poetry* and Ladislav Klíma's

Nemesis the Glorious. Back in 1933 Uncle Standa and Aunt Slávka gave me a Zeiss box camera. It made me an instant king. Even the toughest customers came to attention, arms to their sides, when I aimed my Baby Box at them and said, "Let me take your picture." As often as not I had no film in the camera. All I had to say was that the picture hadn't come out because they'd moved.

40.2. She tried to turn his two children—the young misses, as we called them in Chomutice—against him. Their names were Jarmilka and Jiřinka, and they were spoiled brats. They would turn their noses up at all delicacies placed before them, eating only boiled pea pods sprinkled with salt, a dish we had not heard of at the time. I tried it and found it revolting.

40.3. They lost the land several times: when stamp duties were imposed, when the currency reform took place, and when their institution went bankrupt. But they kept saving. The last disaster hit them in 1935. They had retired by then and never recovered from it.

41.1. The origins of the name reach quite far back. When Chomutice was still a small village, three of its inhabitants chose to build houses on the far side of the pond, thereby forming a kind of unincorporated subvillage or hamlet. It retained the name even after the village began to grow and other houses joined it.

41.2. I loved going to The Hamlet. My cousins and I would play in the attic and hayloft. Uncle Václav enjoyed whipping me with a strap he called "flesh and blood" after the line in a Říha fairy tale that I used to go around shouting at the top of my voice: "Flesh and blood, flesh and blood, I smell human flesh and blood!" Often the thrashings were justified. Once, for instance, I filched some freshly made sausages from a bowl during the annual pig slaughtering. Since I was already full (as Grandmother used to say, my eyes were bigger than my stomach), I took only a few bites and tossed them under the table behind a suitcase. When they were found—there were eight in all—I got a beating. "Just you wait," I said to my uncle. "When I grow up I'm going to be a policeman and put you in jail!"

42.1. The most delicious soft cheese I ever had was during the Second World War on the estate of Karel Vodňanský in Dražičky outside of Tábor. I was working as a forester for the timber company where my Uncle Standa was the chief clerk. Every evening I would go to supper at the house of the Vodňanský family (it was his wood the company was buying) in exchange for giving their son Kárinek violin lessons and tutoring him for the Tábor Gymnasium entrance examination. The meals were excellent: beef, smoked meats, game, fish, mushrooms . . . But after Kárinek failed the exam, I often had the above-mentioned delicacy instead.

44.1. He pulled two of my molars when I was a child. I still dread the smell of iodoform that filled his office. I was also terrified by the human skull grinning up at me from his desk.

45.1. The Dostáls had three children: Jarmila, who played Zulika in the production of *The Strakonice Bagpiper* in which Father played Švanda the Piper, Mother played Kordula, Mirek played Frantík, and I played Honzík; Lola, who married a Jičín butcher; and Láďa, who became a priest in the Czechoslovak Church and wrote poetry, which he published in the Jičín weekly *Krakonoš*. Besides children the Dostáls had a hunting dog they called Héra.

48.1. There are memories, memories of memories, and false memories. As Salvador Dalí says, "The difference between true and false memories is the same as the difference between true gems and paste: the latter are shinier and more authentic-looking" (*The Secret Life of Salvador Dalí*).

49.1. Jindra was my first love. We were in the same class at school, and I loved her in secret and in the open. I once wrote her a love letter—with the salutation "Deer Jindra"—that Joska Budina swiped and mailed, but Postmaster Hradec delivered it, even though it had neither envelope nor address, to my father. This time he refrained from thrashing me and merely gave my ear a tug. All my courting notwithstanding, Jindra remained cool to me, though she did once slip two dozen marbles into my pocket.

49.2. During a "Venetian festival" at the Obora mill-pond in 1929, Mr. Kazda and my father staged a melodrama entitled *The Watersprite*. Father recited the text, and Kazda accompanied him on the piano. It all took place on a raft gliding along the water and propelled by four firemen, who, using a number of planks, had also managed to load the Sokol's upright onto it. A green spotlight trained on the performers heightened the effect and left the firemen on the edges of the raft in darkness.

49.3. He was the first person in town to have a set with five tubes and a speaker, and he made it himself. He also charged batteries for people.

49.4. His wife, Jindra, had had a number of admirers in her youth—estate officials for the most part—but the teacher had triumphed. In addition to being a fine pedagogue, he played the piano, kept bees, and designed and built all kinds of things. He subscribed to a number of both technical and literary magazines. When I was eleven, he began lending me volumes from the Otto edition of the complete historical novels of Alois Jirásek, and I had gone through them all by the time I was fourteen. Then came poetry and Jiří Wolker, whose works my Aunt Albínka lent me in the three-volume Petr edition. (She was Mother's sister and a teacher too, but only ten years older than I was.) My father borrowed Hašek's *Good Soldier Švejk* from the Kazdas, and I was no more than ten the first time I pored over it. But except for a few daring expressions there was nothing in it for me at the time, and I couldn't get over how my otherwise stern father would split his sides with laughter as he read it.

49.5. As boys we enjoyed watching Mr. Kazda in his hood spraying the giant pear of bees that hung from the branch of an apple tree. He would shake it into a swarming box and rummage through it with his bare hand in search of the queen bee.

50.1. Bread and treacle was a much-loved winter dish in peasant families. The treacle was sugarbeet juice reduced on the stove in baking pans to a thick, dark brown syrup. It was stored in five-liter pickling jars. We would pour a little into a bowl and either dip a slice of bread into it or cut it up into smaller pieces and sprinkle them over it, in which case we ate the bread with a fork. We would also drip it onto a kind of bun that had a poppy-seed filling and was steamed and topped with crumbled gingerbread. Then we ate it with a knife and fork or a spoon that had a sharp edge. It was traditional Christmas Eve dinner fare.

50.2. The honeycombs were piled into a kind of spin dryer or honey centrifuge, and their wax caps scraped off. Since a lot of honey stuck to them, we would chew them, and once we had sucked out all the honey, the wax would be melted on the stove and pressed into new honeycomb walls.

52.1. I'd have had a long way to go to school and to play with my friends. But I liked the field with its grassy slope. Besides, it was near the Lužanka, the reed-lined river, where the older boys went for sedge, which they used as stoppers in their pea shooters, and for cat's tails, whose tips we called cigars. See note 30.1.

53.1. Every village had its share of families like theirs at the time. The parents would do seasonal labor on the estate, the children gather grass and clover for the few household rabbits. They were constantly visited by gendarmes investigating thefts of crops and game. And because whole families lived together in a single room, children were initiated early into the details of intimacy. Incest was not infrequent.

54.1. Several other items in the family library came from the same publisher, Kočí: Tomáš Hrubý's multivolume novel *The Twilight of Mankind*, Gustav Pfleger-Moravský's *The Industrialist's Wife*, and Božena Němcová's classic *Granny*.

54.2. *The New People* was a progressive, anticlerical weekly carrying both national and international news. Once a month it contained a literary supplement called "Mead" and devoted to the now completely forgotten poetry of Marie Glabazňová and Zdena Montáňová and stories of Zuzka Zguriška. It was published by the Brno house of František Pokorný, who was the first to bring out Petr Bezruč's important *Songs of Silesia*.

54.3. I did not place much confidence in them because my own penis looked quite different from the one in the illustration. Gentler, I would say.

54.4. He was the son of the onetime Social Democrat and future Communist Čmelík, who would interrupt the speakers with shouts of "Well said!" or "Shame on you!" He had another son by the name of Josef who was a taxi driver in Prague and died on the barricades in May 1945.

54.5. The word occurs in many other songs, which are more scurrilous than obscene. As students we sang a ballad about a Swiss peasant who feels a surge of passion when his wife arrives with a meal in the Alpine meadow he is mowing. But she refuses to do his bidding, pointing out that she has only recently performed her conjugal duty, and so:

> The man begins to shout
> And grabs her by the throat.

A battle ensues:

> She picks up a big stick,
> *In der Schweiz, bei dem Kreuz in Tirol,*
> And whacks his swollen prick,
> *In der Schweiz, bei dem Kreuz in Tirol.*
> With his spade he takes a swat,
> *In der Schweiz, bei dem Kreuz in Tirol,*
> Across her hairy twat,
> *In der Schweiz, bei dem Kreuz in Tirol.*

Where the stick came from or why he needed a spade in the meadow the song doesn't say. Another equally lewd but much longer song in which the word in question figures several times over made the rounds among students when I was young. It was called "In Wenceslas Square" and included this unusual image:

> See that girl neath yonder tree?
> She's still got her cherry.
> Keeps her twat chained up, does she,
> Like a mad dog fierce and hairy.

Or this bittersweet scene that seems to come from an old-age home and uses another taboo term for the female genitalia:

> Two old crones once had a spat
> Over a pat of butter.
> Each grabbed firm her rival's quim
> And roundly jounced the other.

54.6. The Koceks lived in nearby Sobčice. The father was a tailor. There were three sons and two daughters. Milík was the middle son. He attended the school of commerce in Hořice. His elder brother—I no longer remember his name—worked as a salesman in a local shop; his younger brother, Jaromír, studied at the Jičín normal school, then transferred to Prague. He was a good musician, and for a while he conducted the Sobčice church choir. I would help out by singing Jesus in the Passion.

Father gave me a lot of valuable hints, the most important of which was how to bring out the climax of the part, the cry "Eli, Eli, lama zabachthani!"

54.7. Mrs. Hejduková was the daughter of Dr. Urban, the popular doctor who had preceded Dr. Dostál as Chomutice's general practitioner. He died towards the end of the war, but for most of its duration he headed the local provisional military hospital and as such saved many of his patients from being sent to the front. He received considerable bribes and owned four houses, one of which was part of his daughter's dowry when she married Hejduk the teacher. In 1927 the Hejduks moved to Ohrazenice near Turnov. The house was bought by Václav Stich, a grocer and father of my friend Pepík Stich. See note 7.2.

55.1. At the time I observed girls at play and in the water—including babies in prams—with more tension than passion.

55.2. I have long since made my peace with this anatomical phenomenon, boyhood tension eventually turning into adolescent passion. The latter has remained with me to old age, that is, the present.

56.1. From that time on I felt both a constant fear of Father and guilt for an obscure sin I neither conceived nor committed.

57.1. I often heard him state that sparing the rod precluded a proper upbringing. Yet Mirek was never beaten, and I doubt that Father himself (who was not quite twelve when his father died) was ever struck by his mother. I, on the other hand, was spanked with the handle of a long wooden spoon until the age of eighteen. Father claimed that I lied and stole, and he had his reasons. When I was ten, I filched seventy hellers from a jar where we kept ten- and twenty-heller coins for beggars, and used it to buy a Senegalese stamp from Joska Řehák. When Father discovered the crime, he punished and cursed his son the thief. I never got over it. Even now, drifting off, I am visited by the ghosts of my childhood: Stopit, Goaway, Whatareyouuptonow, Leaveitalone, Youdontexpectmetobelievethat, Putthatdowndamnit, Willyoueverlistendamnyou, Dontyoudare, Ivehadenoughofyou, Justyouwait, Youregoingtogetit, Shutupwillyou, Getoutofhere, Waittilldaddycomeshome, Notanotherwordoutofyou, Yourenotgoinganywhere, WhenIsaynoImeanno, Notapeepdoyouhear, Illbeatyoublackandblue, Youlittlebastardyou, Illtearyoulimbfromlimb.

57.2. Even though she did not enjoy the best of reputations, I had no erotic or sexual stake in her. My Eros, resplendent as the feathers in an angel's wing, and my Sex, dark as the hair in the devil's tail, did not celebrate their first triumphs until a year later in the south Boheiman town of Blatná. I spent the summer of 1938 helping to run a children's convalescent home sponsored by the Social Democrats and called The Healthy Generation Sanatorium, and there, on Kaneček Pond, I met and fell madly in love with a local normal school student. We went out four or five times, and I wrote any number of poems to her, one of which bore the title "A Wreath of Evening Stars" and began:

> You are as fair as the skies in wells sown with cilia
> As the skies in the bronze hands of Circe the sorceress
> When she transfigures female corpses into white water lilies . . .

and ended:

> The wreath of evening stars
> Reflected in hoofprint puddles
> And the dew on roses in a secret garden of blood and rain
> Flow on in silence
> To the reeds for which she left me
> To the stones with wild lion eyes I lit for her eyes
> To the mazes from which she will emerge
> Only if led by a blue child at dusk.

We corresponded for a while when we were back at school, but her letters were reserved. I gave her my school address—as I did all the girls I wrote to—because at that age I did not want to seem a Chomutice bumpkin. To each new love I gave Breton's *Nadja* and *Communicating Vases,* Eluard's *Public Rose,* and our own Nezval's *Rue Gît-le-Coeur* and *Prague with Fingers of Rain.* More often than not they sent them back and I never saw the girls again. I also suffered greatly at the thought of how ugly I was. It all began at a restaurant we called the Nople—Hořice's highest-class establishment, the Constantinople—with a girl my own age (we both had three years to go at school). While I tried to clue her in on the difference between Salvador Dalí's paranoic critical method and Max Ernst's *frottages,* her eyes roamed the mirror-studded room. All of a sudden two town swells appeared at the entrance. One said in a loud voice, "Hey, get a load of that smart looker over there!" To which the other replied, "Wonder what she's doing with that turd." I completely lost my train of thought, and my self-esteem plummeted so low that I have no idea how I made it through the evening with her.[1] True, I could write highly lyrical missives, but my Blatná beauty quickly quashed my illusions by losing interest rather quickly, in fact, by putting an end to them in the following missive of her own:

> Dear Friend,
> I hope you will forgive me for taking so long to respond, but a terrible thing has happened: I have broken my right arm. I am doing my best to write, but am having a hard time of it and it is wearing me out something awful. I promise to write more when I can.
> > Yours,
> > Ida L.
> P.S. This took me forty-five minutes to write counting all the pauses.

Blinded by jealousy, I refused to believe her. I sent her one last rather silly letter—more automatic writing than letter, actually—and that was the end of our relationship. Not of my love, however. I stole several of her school's year-end reports from the teachers' library and pined for a month or two over the name of my cruel ideal in the roster. The following summer, back at the Blatná sanatorium (which rented the local school during the holidays), I made friends with the head of the girls' section. She told me that before the Nazis closed the universities she had been studying philosophy, that she had been married and was divorced, and that she was seriously involved with another man. It was she who finally assuaged my sexual longings. Unfortunately, the event provided me with no artistic inspiration whatever. When two months later I received a wedding announcement, I sent the newlyweds an illustrated congratulatory telegram. And thereby the song of a Bohemian youth came to an end.

■ □ ■ □ ■

NOTE TO THE NOTES
TO THE NOTES

(A Coda to *A Bohemian Youth*
dated April 1983)

57.2.1. I met Hanka, the unwilling object of my attempt at
surrealist indoctrination, at a dance in Sylvárův Újezd (popularly
known as Funsville) when I was filling in for Father as bandleader. She picked me as her partner for the first ladies' choice,
and the band—made up of Zdeněk Rosůlka, Mr. Halíř (a.k.a.
Mr. Bristle), Mr. Janďour, Mr. Zmátlík, and my cousin Standa)
accompanied my daring dips with "When They Play the Most
Beautiful Tango." She was a fine-looking girl, well educated and
well heeled (her parents had a large farm—an estate, really), an
orchid among wildflowers. I kept my mind on my feet; she was
the first to speak: "Would you believe there was another fight
here today?" I registered polite surprise. And suddenly she came
out with: "When are you going to have another poem in the
student magazine?" As Vítězslav Nezval put it in his *Prague Pedes-
trian,* I was charmed, I was aroused. But I was also so aflutter that
I could think of nothing more original—when, the music having
come to an end, I took her back to her buxom mother who was
sitting on a bench with the other chaperons—than to thank her
for the dance. The next day, however, I wrote her a note asking

her out. For a week there was no response. Then on 9 May 1939 I received a postcard with a panorama of Kutná Hora: "Best wishes from a short excursion. Yours, Hana." Several of her schoolmates tacked on their signatures. Then she added: "A week or two from Sunday there will be a party at my house. I'm looking forward to talking over your note there." It wasn't easy to get Father to send me back to Funsville—he really wanted me to conduct for him at Třtěnice—but it was worth it: I was overjoyed when Hanka agreed to meet me the following Monday (the summer holidays had just begun) at Ostroměř Pond. Love had burgeoned once more in my heart. We met twice a week: at the pond in the Malé Kabáty woods, at the Lamb Pub in Hořice, or at the above-mentioned Nople. But all good things must come to an end. One day she showed up in Malé Kabáty on a motorcycle or, to be more precise, a ČZ 100 (dubbed "the sputtermobile" by the younger generation). Her parents gave her everything she asked for. I usually went to our dates on Father's old Británia veloci-pede, though Herbert Špigl (see note 7.5) sometimes lent me his racing bike with its inverted handlebars and streamlined seat. I felt humiliated. No, lost. Because my idol had acquired her pas-sion for motorcycles from a certain Karel Fibinger, the proud possessor of a Jawa 250, who had begun taking her on excursions and to local dances. Our friendship limped on for a while, but eventually petered out entirely. She was unmoved by the several poems I dedicated to her, the last of which I even included in my 1942 volume *Lodgings with the Witch of the Night:*

> A rosary of lights, beads said by night,
> Shines, anxious, through the wet landscape.
> White stallions pass along the misty hollow
> Seeking last year's sun, a magic land.
> You may be fast asleep, I am drowsing,
> Wonder burgeoning in the meadows of the eyes.
> Ships of gold sail to us through a sea of darkness;
> Herons of dreams soar to us from the summer.
> We speak again in the wood of sunny whiles;
> The sudden bell of speech rings through the silence.
> Now fingers wander slowly onto breasts,
> And shame conceals your face in its hands.
> A poem made of sleep stays behind in the wood.

You will read it too, I know.
And when the wind shakes autumn into your heart,
A maple leaf will shrivel before my eyes.

Once again my muse proved less than alluring. The Jawa 250 had more to offer. In 1947 I heard she was married, and sometime in 1950 I caught a glimpse of her at the main railway station in Prague. She was standing next to her husband, who looked a good head shorter than she was. Then I completely lost sight of her and never even heard her name until early in March of this year—1983, that is—Pepík Stich (see note 7.2) turned up in Prague. He is living in our native village with his ancient mother, working in a toy shop in Vyoské Veselí to flesh out his pension. Usually he regales me with the details of his still numerous sexual exploits, but this time he took a different tack. "You're not going to believe this!" he said to me. "It'll bowl you over!" "What is it?" "There've been some people asking for you back home, people from Funsville." "Don't tell me my old flame Hanka has gone to her reward." "That's not the half of it: her husband shoved her out of the window!" My wonder knew no bounds. Unfortunately, Pepík could furnish me with no details except that Hanka's married name had been Nováková and that she had lived in Prague, in Holešovice. Before long, however, I was able to read about the tragic end of one of my unhappy loves in two newspaper articles. The first appeared in *Večerní Praha* (Evening Prague) on 3 April 1983:

HE LOVED HER, HE HATED HER

(Prague) I would not have liked to be in the shoes of the men on the bench assigned to hear the case of Jiří N. yesterday afternoon in the Prague Municipal Court. The case was far from simple. It was a case of manslaughter. The tragic event occurred on 8 January in the seventh district. After a restrained but perhaps all the more intense family quarrel over where to spend the summer holidays (Dalmatian Coast or Costa Brava) the sixty-seven-year-old Jiří N. administered several blows to the head of his sixty-one-year-old wife Hana with the iron bar he otherwise used for killing rabbits. He then dragged the corpse out of the windowless bathroom and pushed it through the kitchen window of their fifth-floor flat. The tragedy was over. Taken into custody, the man immediately confessed to the crime. Yet this was not the open-and-shut case it first appeared to be. Jiří N. had spent thirty-seven years of marriage a prisoner to his wife's every whim. He loved her, but her constant harangues made him hate her as well. On that fateful day she had taken him to task for having bought an expensive brand of sauerkraut, and demanded that he return it; she had claimed he used laying flowers on his mother's grave as a front for skirt-chasing; she had yelled at him for spilling water in the bathroom. Jiří N. was driven to the tragic deed by a life of stress. The psychiatrists and psychologists who testified as expert witnesses pointed out that what may have seemed a perfectly normal marriage was in fact riddled with beneath-the-surface conflicts: not only did Hana wear the pants in the family, she held Jiří's more modest origins against him, yet Jiří found it impossible to leave his love-hate relationship. Still, the court had a case of manslaughter before it, and after due consideration it convicted Jiří N. of first-degree murder, sentencing him to seven years imprisonment in a medium-security facility with preventative psychiatric treatment. He will also be required to compensate the Prague 7 Health Authority for 20,000 crowns worth of services rendered. Neither side contested the sentence, which does not yet have the force of law.

The second appeared on the same day in *Svobodné slovo* (The Free Word):

LOVE LEADS TO DEATH

(Prague) For thirty-seven years Jiří N., sixty-seven, lived in a marriage he called happy. And all that time he bore a terrible burden. Not that he felt it. For thirty-seven years he loved his wife Hana, six years his junior. But they had countless spats. Hana never worked, and although her husband supported her he also did the cleaning and shopping. And all he got for his pains was ingratitude. Hana criticized everything about him: his friends— she made him break off with them; his parents—for five years she refused to let him visit their grave; his sister—she forbade him to see her. Then on 7 January she let him pay her a visit—for a short, predetermined time only, of course. The next day he went out to buy some sauerkraut and came back with a jar instead of a plastic bag. She gave him a tongue-lashing. After lunch they discussed their summer plans over a game of cards. She wanted to go to the Dalmatian Coast; he was for Mallorca or Cyprus. He lost. Then she sent him out for some potatoes. Naturally he went. But when he came back, it was like a film in fast motion. She chided him about a mess he had made in the bathroom and accused him, a man of sixty-seven, of using the visit to his sister as a front for "picking up girls." That was the last straw. Beside himself, Jiří N. struck her several times in the head with an iron bar and threw her out of the window. In accordance with §219 of the Penal Code, Jiří N. was convicted yesterday by the Municipal Court of Prague of manslaughter and given a seven-year sentence in a medium-security prison. He will be required to undergo preventative psychiatric treatment. Neither side contested the sentence.

My burlesque *Bohemian Youth* thus ends with an epilogue that makes even *Les Chants de Maldoror* seem a mere rustle of old paper.

■ □ ■ □ ■

WRITINGS FROM AN UNBOUND EUROPE